Heart of
the Hill Country

Follow Your Heart!

Kris J. Klingaman

Heart of the Hill Country

Kris J. Klingaman

She may be reached at *ranchhorsechampion@gmail.com*

Front cover photo provided by the author
Back cover photo and photo on pg.4, Nancy Louden
Photo, pg. 100, KC Montgomery
Photo of Kris and Dave, pg. 101, Jordyn Burco
Show photo, pg. 101, Bar H Photography
Dave and Scooter, pg.102, by Fletch Photography
Dave and Buster, pg. 102, by the author
IQHA, pg. 102, Bar H Photography, Jennifer Horton

Cover design & book layout by Laura Ashton
laura@gitflorida.com

This book is a work of fact, fiction and fantasy. Many of the towns, restaurants and places mentioned in the book are real, and frequented by the author. The names, characters and incidents are either friends of the author that have granted permission for their names to be used, public figures, or the product of the author's imagination and used fictitiously. All horses mentioned are registered with the American Quarter Horse Association, and previously or currently owned by the author. Any resemblance to actual events, persons, living or dead is coincidental.

ISBN: 978-1978306257

Printed in the United States of America

In loving memory of
my dear friend, Deb Kunkle
and a great Paint horse, Dainty Affects, aka Dolly
May you ride together in heaven.

Dedicated to

My Pa ~ Dick Klingaman
Who taught me to set goals, work hard and always have fun.

My Children ~ Josie Lynn and Cord Matthew (aka Digger)
Who always give me motivation and inspiration.
Love you forever!

My Horse ~ Very Smart and Light (aka Pardner)
The most talented horse I've ever ridden

My Love ~ Dave
You hold my heart!

Kris Klingaman with
Very Smart and Light

A portion of the proceeds from this book will go to ASPIRE Therapeutic Horseback Riding, Waterloo, Iowa and the Iowa 4-H Horse Program.

Preface

Cowboys—Cowgirls . . . and cow horses. This action-packed love story will make you kick off your boots, settle into an easy chair, and read cover to cover. Enjoy western drama that leads up to the biggest *World Show Working Cow Horse* ride of a lifetime. So pull your cowboy hat down tight and ride along!

The cowgirl was ready to leave Iowa for many reasons . . . Sick of the weather. Sick of men. Sick of life. It was time to change it all.

Why couldn't she do what she loved? Horses were her true passion. That's where her heart was. That's the dream she had to chase. That's the western lifestyle she yearned for.

Her goal would be riding the best Quarter Horses in the country. She wanted to find a way to utilize horses to make a life- changing impact on others. And most important, she desperately needed someone to share it all with.

Her dream was finding a cowboy who would love her unconditionally with all his heart. A man that would enjoy riding and loving horses as much as she did. A man that would always be true to her, full of deep passion, desire and devotion only for her.

How could any of that *ever* come true?

Saddle up and live the adventure with cowgirl Josie as she rides the Texas trails in search of excitement, with the courage and passion to reach her destiny in the heart of the Hill Country.

Chapter 1

She was ready to get out of Iowa for a number of reasons.

Sick of the weather. Iowa's nothing but hot, miserable, steamy summers of stifling heat and humidity, and winters of bitter cold sub-zero temperatures, ice, blowing snow and blizzards.

Sick of men. Two-faced liars who always say they're not going to hurt her, and end up breaking her heart, taking her pride, her reputation, and her cash when they go.

Sick of life. Working as a secretary at the school to make ends meet and training horses in all other available hours. *Why* couldn't she do what she loved, full time? *Horses were her true passion.* That's where her heart was, that was the dream she had to chase, that was the lifestyle she longed for.

And for years the dream was just "out there." But she vowed that this year would be different.

She had no reason to stay in Iowa now—third divorce, no kids, no permanent home, her only family a brother and sister. All she had there was just a horse barn she rented to train horses out of, and a tiny apartment in the loft. And with times getting tough because of the rotten economy, only a couple of horses at the barn to ride.

She had her own good horse. She had a good dog. She had a pickup truck and a horse trailer. She had enough for a cowgirl to get by, but not to be truly happy.

True happiness…that would be the dream of owning and training the best Quarter and Paint Horses in the country. The dream of having a big ranch with 200 acres, a big ranch house, horse arenas and barns with stalls full of beautiful horses. The dream of riding and winning the prestigious shows and having a world-renowned reputation made from hard work and dedication for her horse training talent and ability. The dream of finding *him*, the cowboy to equal her riding talent, who would worship the ground she walked on, respect and admire her, love her with all his heart and always be true to her. The man who would be good looking, have a great sense of humor, be a great kisser with deep passion, desire and devotion only for her. But, of course it was all just a dream.

How could any of that ever come true?

Jo, whom friends referred to as Josie, set the date—two weeks from today. She had loose ends to tie up. She had to notify the owners and send home the three training horses she had. She had to let the barn owner know she was pulling out. She had to pack and load her few possessions, and say goodbye to her best girlfriends. But this was it. The decision was made. She was headed for Texas on March 30.

She wasn't quite sure where, but Josie had friends of friends living down there, and she could only hope someone needed a ranch hand, groomer or stall picker. Lord knows Texas folks wouldn't recognize her as a trainer, coming from Iowa. Texans knew horses, and they knew *authentic* cowboys and cowgirls by the way they talked, by the way they shaped their hat and mostly by the way they rode. They *thought* no good horse trainers came from Iowa. The Midwest was full of farmers and corn country…who knew how to ride up there? Josie hoped to prove them wrong.

Josie's best friend was her Welsh Corgi. Maverick was a tri-color; he had a mostly black body with white legs, copper-brown face markings, and inner ear hair. He'd been with Josie for eight years. Faithful, loving, quiet Corgis were cow dogs, a herding type of quick, smart, short legged furballs of fun. Maverick was happiest whenever he was with Josie— riding in the truck with her, watching her ride horses, or just lying in the house, he usually had one eye on Josie. She loved her dog. He was an important part of her life and stability.

Her girlfriends couldn't believe she was really going to do it. Sierra and Marne, pure Iowa cowgirls and best friends growing up, had always been there to pick up the pieces when Josie shattered after another love gone bad.

Sierra was a 26-year-old barrel racer. *Turn and burn* was her motto, for barrel racing or where men were concerned. "Can't live with 'em, can't live without 'em," she'd say. So, she did both. A different cowboy every week never seemed to bother her. In fact, that was the challenge she liked. She ran the rodeo circuit all over the Midwest with a fast palomino Quarter Horse. She was a long-legged, tall drink of water, a perfectly built woman. Standing 5'10", with a tight blouse, tighter jeans and wearing a big silver belt buckle she'd won, she'd get all the cowboys smiling at her when she'd talk about how fast she was…on and off her horse.

"Going to the rodeo," she would say, "is just like going to the grocery store and picking out whatever you want. See all those good-looking cowboys sitting on that fence over there…just pick out whose boots ya want under your bed tonight." Josie could only shake her head at Sierra.

"Ain't no way to live, girl," Josie would forewarn. "You're gonna end up diseased, pregnant, lonely…or all three!"

"Naaaaa," Sierra would say. "I'm gonna end up with the best stories to tell in the old people's home when I'm 95, and the spur notches in my bed post to prove it! Cowgirl up, Josie, and join me. I'll even give you first pick!"

"Oh noooo, I ride a pleasure horse, slow and easy and one good one is *all* I need!" Josie would say.

Sierra would just laugh. "Suit yourself…your loss, Jos."

Marne didn't share Sierra's lifestyle or attitude. A cutie, a petite 25-year-old, with reddish-blonde hair, her style of horses and men were the classics. She went for the foundation breeding, good toplines, conformation, and most important, disposition. A bit of a gold digger, Marne's criteria in men was that they must have hair, teeth and cowboy boots. In the last few years she added financial security to the list, too. Since hanging around with Sierra and learning that many of the rodeo cowboys lacked all her desired criteria, Marne stuck to breed shows with her Quarter Horses. That was where the "big time" cowboys resided.

Big, brand-new, fancy horse trailers and pickup trucks, expensive cowboy hats and boots, starched jeans and shirts, deluxe silver saddles and bridles, quality high priced horses—this was more of the financially

9

stable horse crowd. Not that many of them actually earned the money by training. Most of it had been earned at their high-paying town jobs or came from a family inheritance. But Marne didn't care where the money came from—just that it was there, and she got a piece of it.

The common bond for Josie Lynn and her best friends was trust. The three grew up together, went to the same school and 4-H Club and FFA, and always had shared a love of horses. Girls and horses...just seem to go together. They all had several horses to show and learn on while growing up. Although the three went in different directions for show circuits in their twenties, they always came back home at the end of a weekend, to talk horses and cowboys.

Josie, 26, was a 5'9" slim-built brunette who was never without her cowboy boots and her Corgi dog. With a bubbly, outgoing personality, and good work ethic, she was not one to shy away from any job, no matter how dirty or hard. Her biggest fault was always believing that what people said was true. Especially when it came to cowboys. She fell in love with each one who was nice to her...then they took what they wanted and moved on. Her lengthy *Losers List*—what her friends called their ex's—included an artist cowboy. Such a big talker about how he was going to paint and sculpt. He made a few pencil sketches and fancy drawings. He did have talent, but mostly he liked holding down the couch and polishing his cowboy boots. He took a job hanging gutters, with no intention of encouraging her show aspirations.

Husband number two was a tall drink of water, liked to hunt and fish, talked about taking her to all the big shows and buying her great horses. He got a factory job and decided beer drinking with his friends was lots more important than horse shows. And when he started complaining and bitching about how much a new headstall and bit cost...she'd had enough.

The last bad choice had a temper, but he sure could ride a horse. She figured they had the common link of horse affairs. Affairs, yes. But not the kind she planned. He had an affair—with another cowgirl. Thank goodness Sierra got wind of it. She tailed him one night, then told Josie all the details. Marriage over.

Josie Lynn was a beautiful girl, and a hell of a hand with a horse. Fate had just dealt her some bad cards up to this point, but she was ready to change all that now. Nearly broke after divorce number three, she was ready to sacrifice her showing and get a fresh start. She would miss showing, though. Through her years of horse showing she had State Quarter Horse Champions, Circuit Champions and State Fair Champions and wins all over Iowa in many associations and saddle clubs. She'd competed in nearly every event including speed events, halter and pleasure classes, but her favorite events had always been reining and working cow horse.

Reining is a unique chorography of horse and rider doing spins, 30-foot sliding stops, lead changes and speed changes from slow pleasure lope to nearly out of control, full-speed gallop. When working a cow, the horse has the advantage of being in control. At the same time, the horse should exhibit a smooth willingness to do his job. He should respond to a light rein and show good manners at all times. It takes years to train a horse, and most good trainers have had at least 15 years of riding under their belts.

Josie loved the horsemanship required to ride a good reiner and cow horse, but she also loved the people on the show circuit. These were the most genuine, honest folks going. They built life-long friendships, they cheered for each other at the shows, and they welcomed new riders into the events. They had all the fancy trucks and trailers with bells and whistles. But there just was not the emphasis to have all the show-off stuff. Heck, if someone pulled into the show in a little old truck and trailer with a really good horse, everyone at the show would welcome them, visit with them and encourage them to come back again. They were competitive and wanted to win, but they wanted good friendships and good horses more. They didn't rush their colts in training, just took their time, so the horses loved the sport just like the cowboys and cowgirls did. Just friendly, good folks that loved their horses and their cows.

But Josie was ready to leave all that love of showing—and her painful trail of husbands and boyfriends—in Iowa to head for real life in Texas. She was ready to leave the good and the bad. She was ready to leave the wicked heat and shivering cold…she'd give it all up…just to chase the dream. The Texas dream. It was time.

Chapter 2

Marne had a friend of a friend in Texas who needed a groomer. Not much experience was necessary, just know how to hold a brush and be willing to spend hours brushing horses, and throwing saddles on to get horses ready for the trainer to ride.

Pay was $250 a week plus a one-bedroom cabin to live in. When Josie inquired about the job and said that she was interested, but wanted to bring her horse and dog, the ranch manager told her, "No way," on the horse, but the dog could come. Josie decided to leave her Paint mare in Iowa with Heathar. She owned a boarding stable; she would take excellent care of the mare, show her some, use her for lessons for little kids to learn to ride, and genuinely love her until Josie could make arrangements to come back and get her. Could be a month, could be 10 years. Heathar was fine with that. Josie left her trailer too, in case Heathar needed to use it.

Josie called ranch manager Bob Campbell back, and told him she'd take the job. "Be there in two days." One last night with Sierra and Marne and several blenders full of Margaritas, and Josie had heard all the philosophy and good wishes she could stand. She hugged her best friends goodbye, put her tired, spinning head on her pillow for what seemed like minutes, and woke up to a wicked-loud alarm clock that meant it was time to go.

She threw the last few items in, called the Corgi to take his place on the passenger's seat, jumped in the driver's seat of her red Chevy truck and away they went on I-35 southbound, never looking back in the rear-view mirror. She had finally done it.

A hard drive with lots of traffic, she made it to south of Oklahoma

City, got a motel room and a peaceful night's sleep, the tri-colored Corgi by her side—her favorite bed partner, and now life partner.

"Hope I'm taking us in the right direction, Maverick," Josie whispered as she kissed his head goodnight.

Next day she awoke and welcomed bright orange sun. She and the dog jumped out of bed, got in the truck and continued south on Interstate 35 to Austin, Texas, where she took a turn west on highway 290 headed for Fredericksburg, Texas. A good eight-hour drive, she got in around 6 p.m.

She pinched herself as she approached the ranch entrance. The huge gate with an overhead entrance sign said Dream Catcher Ranch. Texas stars hung on boulders, big yucca plants, cactus and green shrubs; life-size bronze horse statues reared in the areas on both sides of the massive entryway. Driving slowly, she proceeded up the road. The private ranch drive was lined with three vertical rows of white pipe fence on both sides, following the winding road.

And trees everywhere! Large, old, live oak trees, mesquite trees, evergreen trees and some she didn't know quite what they were. But it smelled good. It smelled like pine. It seemed like forever to reach the actual ranch barns. Must have been a full mile of road and fence. Since it was still daylight, she could see the big pastures of lush green grass and horses inside the pipe fence—lots and lots of horses, some Quarters, some Paints. There must have been 30 to 40 head in each pen. Some were yearlings, some probably two-year-olds. Farther up the drive, she crossed a wooden bridge over a small creek, made two more sharp curves in the road, all with the white pipe fence still running alongside. She saw a pasture of broodmares and babies. Big, heavily muscled, soggy mares. She could tell immediately they were quality bred, powerful—good Quarter Horses.

She reached the horse barns, parked her truck and stepped out, trying not to look like a hick just out of Iowa. The barns were massive. She saw a beautiful, huge, show stall barn, outdoor arena, indoor arena, many dry-lot pens and a mare motel with new, silver pipe stalls and a green tin roof overhead. Josie was wondering if she'd just crossed over to heaven.

"Howdy, ma'am, can I help you?" A tall, twenty-year-old cowboy stepped out of the show barn heading for his pickup parked nearby with a blonde in the passenger seat.

"*Oh*, yes, I'm Josie from Iowa, the new groomer."

"Ohhhhh, sure 'nuf, ma'am, make yourself at home in the little cabin back yonder. Mr. Bob will meet with ya in the morning, 7 a.m. sharp. And my name is Digger, Digger Matthews, the assistant trainer."

"Pleased to meet ya, Digger," Josie declared as she jumped back in her truck. Admiring his sexy southern drawl, she drove to the nearby grove of trees where one cabin and two trailer houses were located.

Music was blaring out of one trailer house with an older S10 pickup parked out front. Josie pulled her truck up to the cabin; she had to stop and listen a few minutes, not quite sure of the tune. *Oh, duh,* she thought, *it's Spanish I'm hearing. Mexicans must be here, too. Hope they make a good Margarita, and maybe they know where to buy the best nacho chips and salsa in town.*

She started unloading the truck, carrying two suitcases into the cabin with Maverick close behind. She opened the door, and to her surprise here was a gorgeous—but tiny—home. She walked into the kitchen that opened into the living room with a wood burning stove in the corner. Floors and walls were a fresh, clean, knotty pine; open rafters with big beams of wood crossed the ceiling with a fan mounted in the peak of the roof. A big, red, woven Navajo rug lay on the living room floor; the couch and chair were log furniture with western bucking horses on red fabric on the back and seat. *This is awesome,* she thought. The kitchen, with plenty of cupboards and appliances, even had a small island made of knotty pine with two pine stools and countertops of concrete colored stone.

She checked out the bedroom and bath, all furnished with rustic log furniture and antler light fixtures. It was just so *western*. It was just so *Texas*. She loved it. For the first time in a long time, she felt good about her decision, and about herself. A couple more loads hauled in, she collapsed into bed, the Corgi next to her, both snoring in a matter of minutes.

Chapter 3

Josie's alarm went off at 5 a.m. She was not going to miss any part of this day—her first day on the job at Dream Catcher Ranch. Famous for its well-bred, prize-winning Quarter and Paint Horses, Dream Catcher Ranch was owned by the Sutcliffs, Alan and Nikky.

The couple was in their early thirties. Alan grew up the son of a rancher, and had had a modest, hard-working upbringing. Well-educated at Texas A&M, following graduation Alan and a partner speculated on a chain of run-down Texas barbecue restaurants, turned them into upscale and chic country-western meccas, then sold them for millions. Following his windfall, he met Nikky through friends that thought he needed eye-candy on his arm. Through pressure from friends and family, they married after just three months of dating.

The first six months of their now four-year marriage, Nikky was sweet, eager to learn the horse business; she was well-liked. As the marriage progressed, Nikky changed. She became more demanding in her presence at the barn, belittled Alan in front of friends, frequented numerous credit card limits for frivolous wants, and became moody and short-tempered. Most days she slept until noon, went out to mid-afternoon lunch or happy hour, then painted for an hour on her antique carousel horse collection, then arrived at the barn demanding a riding lesson just as the work day was ending for Bob and Digger. The barn help constantly had to put their supper and evening plans on hold so that "Queen Nikky," as they secretly nicknamed her, could have her barn time. Her lack of respect for nearly everyone became more apparent as time went by.

Josie reached the barn door at 6:45 a.m. She wanted to be early to make a good first impression. She was dressed in good-fitting wranglers, an Iowa State tee shirt, and Ariat boots. Her long hair was pulled back in a ponytail, cascading down her shoulders and back. A slim 120 pounds, she looked like a cowgirl ready to tackle the tasks of the day. She met Bob, an older, weathered-face cowboy, skin so dark he could be Indian or Mexican, smoking a cigarette as they did introductions.

"Oh, you must be the new gal…. Glad to meet ya, Miss Josie," Bob shouted. "I've been needing a good groomer. Damn Mexicans are only good for cleaning stalls; ain't none of them know how to really brush a horse."

One of the Mexicans, Pedro, popped his head out of a stall, where he'd been picking and overheard the comment. He fingered Bob and cursed in Spanish.

"¡Andale! ¡Andale!" Bob yelled back, laughing. *"Hey,* just clean the damn stall!" Bob turned to Josie and joked, "They should'a learned English before they came up here, but damn I can say all kinds of shit to them and they don't have a clue. Plus, I love their food. Hey, Miss Josie, come on, I'll show you around."

Bob gave Josie the tour of the barn. It was fabulous, like nothing she's ever seen before—big, paved, wide alleyway between 30 box stalls. The stall fronts were knotty pine wood slats on the bottom half, steel vertical bars on the top half, for easy viewing of every horse. Each stall had a big sliding door to go into the stall, as well as a small door that opened for easy access to the feeder. The stalls were full of horses bedded deep in white, fresh, pine wood shavings. Big ceiling fans ran the length of the alleyway to circulate air. The smell was incredibly fresh, not at all like there was any livestock in it. At the end of the alleys were large, roll-up, overhead doors, already open on this beautiful 70-degree spring morning. Horses were munching on their grain, while another Mexican—Bob introduced him as Chico—was pushing a big, squeaky-wheeled cart down the alley, opening and slamming the stall feed doors, putting bright green hay into each stall.

Bob showed her the office. Glass French doors opened to a massive room with a huge oak desk and chair. Trophy shelves were loaded with World and Futurity Champion trophies and ribbons, and other trophies of every shape and size. Large, lit, oil paintings of horses hung on one wall, with bronze name plaques below the pictures. It was quite overwhelming, and fabulous. Josie pinched herself when Bob wasn't watching. She was still amazed at all she had encountered in the last two days. Bob took Josie to show her his smaller office, the tack room and the wash rack. They took a quick glance at the arenas and mare motel, which was full of mares with babies in stalls for breeding later to one of the two Sutcliff stallions.

Bob pointed to a mansion of a ranch house on the hilltop overlooking the entire ranch. "That's where the boss man and the missus reside, and my shack is to the north of that, beside the head trainer, Steve Jackson's place, the mini mansion up there.

"Wow, this place sure has lots of folks living on it!" Josie replied.

"You'll meet them all soon enough, Miss Josie. Just let me know if you have any questions. You just answer to me. You don't have to take no crap from anyone else. Somedays this place has too many chiefs and not enough Indians...." Bob went on, "I'll take good care of you. You seem like a nice, Midwest-kinda gal."

Josie wasn't quite sure what that meant...but she said, "OK, Bob, whatever you say."

They ended up back at the main barn where Bob showed Josie which horses he wanted her to begin working on.

"Pull out that dun mare, clean her up and saddle her so she's ready for Steve when he stumbles down here."

"Sure thing, Bob," Josie says.

Going in the stall, she talked to the dun in a calm voice. The mare turns and looked at her with ears up and big soft eyes.

"Oh, you are a sweetheart, aren't you? We're gonna get along just fine," Josie said to her. She got her haltered, and took her out in the alleyway, put her in the crossties, and began to brush. An hour later, with sawdust shavings, hair and dirt covering the floor under the mare, Josie had her brushed and saddled as Bob walked by.

"Looking good...get another," Bob responded in a cheerful voice.

Josie continued the routine, having two more horses groomed and saddled as she heard a commotion near the barn door.

"Who the hell left that Ranger in my way?" demanded the booming voice.

Bob answered back, "The same asshole that said you were a good horse trainer."

"Oh, shut the hell up, old man!" was the nasty reply.

It seemed the trainer, Steve, had stumbled into the Polaris Ranger that Bob drove.

Steve walked right past Josie, looked at her, but said nothing. His spurs jingled with every step he took. The barn got strangely quiet all of a sudden. She smelled a strong scent of whiskey as he passed her. *God, she thought, is he drunk at 11:00 in the morning?*

Steve made his way into the tack room, grabbed a bridle, went up to the dun mare and attempted to bridle her with fumbling fingers.

"What the hell is the matter with this headstall?" Steve asked.

No one answered.

Finally, he got the mare bridled and led her out to the arena and mounted up.

He rode her nicely the first ten minutes, then he began jerking the reins, putting pressure on the bit, harder and harder. The mare ducked her chin to her chest, began wringing her tail and getting upset. Steve jerked harder, until the mare was in a near frenzy. She was trying her best to please him and do what he commanded, but he wasn't happy with anything she did. In a short time, the mare was lathered with sweat on her neck, shoulder and flank. Her brain was fried. Steve jerked her to a stop, stepped off and put her in the stall with her saddle and bridle still on; he tied her head tight with the rein to the girth of the saddle. She was curving her neck back to the saddle so much it looked like it would snap.

"There, bitch, think about that," Steve sneered.

Then he slammed the stall door, just to watch her flinch and jerk her sore mouth where the bit was tied with a tight rein.

Steve went to the office to answer a phone call. Josie caught a glance at Bob as he walked by the dun mare's stall, just shaking his head.

Steve yelled out from the office, "Have Digger ride the rest of my horses. I'm going to San Antonio to look at a couple pleasure mares."

He jumped in a new dually pickup—grabbing a brown paper sack under the seat as he got in—and took off.

Bob got on his cell phone and made a call to Digger, who'd been out checking colts in the big pasture.

"Get your ass up here boy, got some horses to ride!" Bob yelled.

In a matter of minutes, Digger was in the barn, nearly ran to the tack room, grabbed a bridle and raced to the arena with one of the horses Josie had ready to go.

Digger lunged the Paint gelding about ten minutes before stepping on. A practice that Digger had learned from good trainers, he would stand at the center of a circle with a long lead rope attached to the gelding's halter, and the colt would go around Digger in circles. This was a great way to get the play out of the colt and tire him down a bit, without having to get in a fight with him correcting bad behavior.

Digger's logic was that most every horse wants to go out and run and buck and play, just like kids do before they go to school. By getting rid of that excess energy, they could concentrate when you wanted to teach them something. Josie bet that logic worked perfectly on horses and kids.

After ten minutes of lunging the Paint gelding, going both directions at a walk, jog and lope—with a few bucks in between—the colt was ready to ride. Digger removed the halter and gently put on the bridle, using a ring snaffle training bit.

Josie peeked out to watch Digger ride. He was a good rider. Patient, with steady hands and soft cues, he was much more impressive to watch than Steve, Josie thought. The horse listened and was so willing to learn as Digger went through a series of maneuvers. Josie decided right then who was the better horse trainer.

Bob directed Josie, "Better take care of the mess Stevie left," pointing to the dun mare's stall.

Josie knew just what he meant. She went quietly in the dun mare's stall, gently untied the rein that was cramping her neck and pulling her face around to the girth. That released the pressure so the mare could straighten her neck and back. *In the right circumstance, this is an effective training tactic*, Josie thought, *but not to this mare*. This mare was special. She didn't deserve this kind of treatment; this would break her spirit and make her worthless as a show horse and even as a decent riding horse.

Josie quietly led the mare out of the stall, unsaddled her, and removed her bridle, noticing the blood coming from the sores in the corners of her mouth with traces on the bit. She put her halter on her and led the mare to the wash rack, giving her a soothing warm bath, talking in a calm, comforting tone of voice, all the time while washing the mare. The mare seemed much more relaxed and quiet by the end of the bathing. Josie washed and conditioned her black tail, then braided it with a rubber band at the end to ensure it would stay long, soft and beautiful. This mare was special. She deserved special care.

Chapter 4

The days at Dream Catcher came and went, very similar to the first day. Steve was a drunk, that was easy to see. He may have been a fair trainer back in the day, or at least cared enough to try to train with good horsemanship skills, but that was long gone. He was a burned-out, burnt-up, spoiled brat of a cowboy, trying to still make it on his reputation. Everyone close to him knew exactly what he'd become.

Most of the horses on the ranch with show records were bought that way. It wasn't that Steve had made them champions, he just had the Sutcliffs buy them after other trainers had wins on them. Then he could get on and win more.

Alan wasn't the driving force behind buying any of the famous winning horses; it was Nikky. And she loved to have everyone know how much of Alan's money she'd spent paying for them. $50,000 for one mare, $300,000 for a stallion, $20,000 for a pleasure mare. She would always tell listeners what each horse cost. Sometimes she would consult with Steve before making a purchase, other times, she'd just buy one, only to find out when it got home it was a disaster—some overpriced idiot of a horse that a seller just made look good, when it was really a counterfeit. Nikky did not know horses. She thought she did. God, she thought she knew everything about horses, ranches and men. Nothing was further from the truth.

Josie first met Nikky when she came down to the barn for a riding lesson. It was 5:30 p.m., when all the barn help had been working since 6 or 7:00 a.m. Everyone was dog tired and ready to leave, and Nikky would walk in and demand to get her lesson. Because Steve was usually gone by then—probably drinking somewhere—Digger ended up having to give the lesson to Nikky. Bob was out in the mare motel, finishing up for the day.

Digger pulled out Bozo, a kid-broke old chestnut gelding, from his stall and began to saddle him, as Nikky strolled by. "Oh, are you the new stable girl?" she asked Josie.

"Yes, ma'am," Josie replied.

"Well, get my mounting steps then!" Nikky demanded.

"Your what?" Josie awkwardly asked.

"My mounting steps in the tack room. Take them to the arena for me to get on!" Nikky ordered.

Josie did as she was told, and couldn't believe it, as Digger took Bozo to the arena, led him up to the steps and Nikky had to climb them to get up in the saddle, onto the horse. Josie glanced at Digger and rolled her eyes. Digger looked away so he wouldn't laugh. Josie never saw someone use steps to get on a horse before.

Although Josie had seen photos of Nikky in the office, a petite woman when Alan married her—she wasn't anymore. Wide in the pockets and thunder in the thighs, Nikky had to be close to 220 pounds. And the horse knew it. Bozo was patient and kind, but his back sagged lower as Nikky, finally astride, gave him a big kick in the ribs. She bounced in the saddle as he trotted around the arena.

Josie watched the riding lesson from a shadow near the end of the barn. Digger was coaching his best, Bozo was performing his best, but Nikky wasn't happy. "What's the matter with this stupid horse?" she challenged.

Digger replied, "Just give him more rein, ma'am; he'll drop his head and slow down." As Josie observed, the longer Nikky rode, the more she dug her heels into Bozo's sides.

"Try and relax your leg and heel, Nikky," Digger would calmly say. She didn't. Bozo, feeling the pressure, just trotted faster and faster until it was a commotion of butt slapping in the saddle, arms and reins waving in the air, a pissed off horse and a mad woman.

Nikky pulled Bozo into the middle and stopped. "Bring my steps, dammit!" Nikky demanded. Digger obliged. Nikky stepped off, pouting and went back to her SUV, the black Cadillac Escalade parked right outside the office and left for the house.

"Well, that was a quick ride," Josie stated to Digger, waiting for his reaction.

"Yeah, it usually is," he replied.

Just then Bob came in from finishing chores in the mare motel. "Oh…is Miss Nikky coming down to ride?" Bob asked.

"She's already been here and done left," Digger answered.

Bob chuckled, "That didn't take long…typical." Bob said goodbye to Josie and Digger as he left the barn to go eat supper.

Digger was the bright spot in Josie's days. He always had a smile, a joke and sometimes they'd have a beer together sitting outside the barn after work. He was more like a brother to her than anyone had ever been. He had a serious girlfriend, which was okay, because Josie wasn't looking for any of that anyway; he was just a hardworking, southern cowboy who was fun to hang out with. And he could ride. Josie knew he was just at Dream Catcher Ranch as an apprentice to build up his reputation and make friendships with Sutcliff's friends. So if and when he did go to training on his own, he'd probably have some owners lined up that would send him horses to train.

"Hey, Jos, wanna beer?" Digger invited.

"Oh, hell ya!" Josie exclaimed. He grabbed a couple cold longnecks from a small refrigerator hidden in the back of the tack room, and they made their way outside to the back of the barn to find a couple of buckets to turn over and sit on to enjoy their cold Lone Star beers.

"So, what do ya think of the place so far, after a couple weeks?" Digger asked.

"Wow, that's a good question," Josie stammered. "In my opinion, you're the one who should be doing all the training! Steve's nothing but a drunk, the boss lady is cold, mean and clueless when it comes to riding, Bob's a good shit and he works hard…he makes the place go, and those Mexicans make one damn fine margarita." Josie rattled on.

"Bahahahahahaha!" Digger laughed so hard he nearly fell off his bucket.

"But, I'm amazed that I haven't met the boss man yet," Josie continued.

"Well, none of us has seen much of him lately," Digger responded. "Rumor has it he's pretty miserable with the missus turning into such a piranha. He probably never should have married her; he had a good life before, 'cept all his friends kept telling him he was missing something, and he went and believed 'em. Thought this Nikky woman was going to enhance his life," Digger went on. "Oh, she enhanced the shit out of it. She offended most of his friends, she tries to control him, she spends his money like there's a money tree growing out back. She's just mean, probably 'cause she's so unhappy with herself."

Digger continued. "The way I see it, those filthy rich people that don't make the money, they're ones that just marry into the money or inherit big money—they're just never really happy inside. They constantly look to buy something to make them happy, but it never does. It's just a vicious cycle.

"But the boss man—Mr. Alan—he's different," Digger continued. "He's made all the money himself. He worked hard, growing up ranching and farming with his daddy on a pretty poor ranch, from what I've heard. Alan put himself through school, made some good business deals and earned all the money he's got. He knows what it is to be happy, or at least he did 'til he married Nikky.

"Hey, Jos, you want another cold one?" Digger wondered.

"Nahhhh, guess I've had enough." Josie replied, laughing. "I can tolerate the fricking loud music those Mexicans play every night now. But I can't understand a dang word!" She hesitated, and in a serious tone continued, "It just seems so sad though."

"What's that?" Digger questioned.

"That Alan has worked so hard for all this, and can't even enjoy it. Such a beautiful ranch, incredible horses and facility," Josie declared.

"Yeah, guess you're right" Digger replied. "Oh well, such is life," Digger went on, "Ya make your bed, ya lie in it, my Daddy always said."

"Guess so," Josie answered.

"Hey, wanna go uptown with my girlfriend Jaclyn and me?" Digger invited. "There's plenty to do there."

"Sounds fun!" Josie exclaimed "Give me 10 minutes to clean up!"

Chapter 5

Changed into stretch-tight Wrangler jeans, a close-fit tiny brown t-shirt, bling belt and Justin boots, and a quick brush of her hair, Josie jumped in Digger's gray Chevy pickup; winding down the ranch road, they were headed for town. Digger's 2008 truck had every bell and whistle possible on it, leather seats, surround sound, tool box in the back, plus a big cattle guard of bars protecting the front headlights and grill.

"Nice truck," Josie complimented.

"Yeah, every good cowboy has to have a good truck," Digger replied. "It's just the Texas way." He reached back to a cooler in the backseat and grabbed two Lone Star beers. "This is the Texas way, too," Digger said.

"I like Texas tradition," Josie declared as she eagerly grabbed one of the beers.

Hill Country was beautiful. She'd noticed that the day she drove down from Iowa. The curved roads would twist and wind around the gorgeous hills and valleys like the road would never come to an end.

She and Digger made their way to town, driving on narrow Old San Antonio Road, a series of giant hilltops with vistas of panoramic views of tree tops and distant hills. Feeling like she was on a roller coaster ride, they would twist up and up, turn after turn, this way then that, reach the peak, grab a few seconds of that twenty-mile-a-way view of blue hazed hills, then straight down, more curves and turns down, down until bump…as they crossed a dip in the road going over a small stream below. And the road trip continued all over again, sometimes crossing narrow bridges, sometimes narrow blind corners when Josie just prayed no one was coming from the other direction. Sometimes at the top of the hill she couldn't even see the road below them and wasn't even sure it was there for a split second, until—*wheeeew*—finally the road reappeared. But she was in Texas and she loved it. She was happy and having fun for the first time in many years.

"So, Digger, you must have grown up in Texas?" Josie inquired.

"Well, yeah, right here in Fredericksburg," Digger replied. "I love the Hill Country" he continued. "It's home, and the prettiest place on earth, far as I can tell.

"Lots of good horses and Longhorns," he went on "the best country music anywhere, and lots of cute cowgirls and cold beer!"

"Oh, yeah, I agree on most all that," Josie confirmed.

Digger went on to tell Josie about his girlfriend Jaclyn that was going to college and worked part time at the bakery in town, as they pulled up to her family's ranch to pick her up.

"Jump in, Jaclyn, and meet Josie, the new ranch hand." Digger introduced them as he grabbed three cold Lone Stars.

As the girls got acquainted and made small talk about the weather, Digger cranked the tunes on the surround sound truck radio.

"Mamas, don't let your babies grow up to be cowboys..." Digger sings along with the Willie Nelson song blaring on the CD *"...don't let 'em play guitars and drive them old trucks, make 'em be doctors and lawyers and such."*

Finally, all three in the truck sing along... *"Mamas don't let your babies grow up to be cowboys; they'll never stay home, they're always alone, even with someone they lovvvvve."*

Josie never knew life could be so fun and so beautiful! She wasn't missing her friends back home anymore; she'd made new friends, good friends here in Texas. *Digger was right,* she thought, *this is the prettiest place in the country.* But she also thought she better keep that a secret, or most of Iowa would want to move down here!

They got to highway 290, took a left turn to head straight into town.

"So, where we going?" Josie inquired.

"Hondo's!" both Digger and Jaclyn yelled at the same time.

"Oh yeah? What's the story on Hondo's?" Josie questioned.

Jaclyn filled her in. "Hondo was the good old cowboy who really made Luckenbach famous. Well, Hondo and his friends Jerry Jeff

Walker and Willie Nelson. You Yankees have heard of Luckenbach, haven't ya?"

"Well, hell, yes!" Josie boasted.

"Well," Jaclyn continued, "Hondo also started a great country bar uptown here with live country music nearly every night of the week. Even though old Hondo is gone, his daughter runs the place and it's one of the best joints in Fredericksburg."

"Awesome!" said Josie.

They pulled up to the old stone building, walked in through the patio area to a wonderful old country saloon. Straight ahead, there was a big stone fireplace, with a huge painting of Hondo hanging on it. Many other pictures of Hondo hung throughout, even a life-size poster of him stands right next to the stage. The stage area, on Josie's left, just big enough for the four-man band that was setting up, was lined with beer boxes along the walls up on the stage with the band, probably stacked six feet high. To her right, there was a huge, dark walnut, old western saloon bar as long as half the room. Behind it a giant mirror reached to the ceiling, with shelves along both sides of the mirror. The tables were old round wooden tables, perfect card playing size, with oak captain's chairs. All the pictures of Hondo were a weathered wrinkly-faced old cowboy with white hair and beard, a dusty beat-up old cowboy hat, wearing a blue chambray shirt and blue jeans. Nothing fancy. Just the real deal. He was Western, and so was his namesake bar.

The three sat down at a table near the bar, with Digger grabbing menus from the bar and ordering three Lone Stars as they walked in. "So, what's good to eat here?" Josie probed.

"Most everything, but the specialties are the Hondo doughnut burger, the brisket and the homemade curly fries and tater chips," Digger answered. "Orders are placed at the bar, and you pick up your food in the kitchen when it's ready, just like home."

It wasn't more than a few minutes after they placed the order that the food was ready. Josie bit into her doughnut burger…it was delicious. A huge hunk of burger, its extra-sweet good flavor reminded her of meatloaf. There was supposed to be a hole in the middle—like a doughnut—on that toasted bun, but she ate it so fast who would know. It was delicious. Homemade curly fries served in a can, were out of this world good with taste and crispness.

27

As they finished supper, the band started playing. Most of the crowd jumped up and went for the small dance floor to do the Texas two-step. Josie was impressed. *What good dancers these Texans are*. Pretty soon Digger and Jaclyn decided to dance too, spinning and twirling all while doing a perfect two-step. *Looks like they've been doing this their whole lives…they make it look so easy.*

One local cowboy spied Josie sitting alone, went up and grabbed a chair beside her and sat down.

"Pretty cowgirl shouldn't be sitting all alone…that's just wrong. How about a dance, sweetheart?" the cowboy inquired.

"Well, not sure if I know that two-step thing," Josie says.

Cowboy snorted, "Guess that means you didn't grow up in Texas… but I'll teach ya just the same. C'mon, little lady."

Josie reluctantly got up and they made their way to the little dance floor in front of the stage.

"Lead with the right…drag the left for two steps, then lead with the left foot and drag the right, easy as pecan pie," Cowboy snickered.

Right, drag, right, drag, left, drag…by cracky, I've got it, Josie told herself.

"See, told ya you'd catch right on, just like riding a bike…what ranch you been hiding out on anyway, missy?" Cowboy asked as they danced. "And by the way, my name's Tim."

"I'm working at the Dream Catcher," replied Josie, as Tim gave her a spin.

"Told ya you'd pick this up. Where the heck ya from?" he asked.

"I'm from Iowa," Josie replied.

"You can't be training at Dream Catcher, are ya grooming or picking?" Tim asked.

"I'm grooming," Josie said, "but it's too bad all you Texans think only southerners can ride…there are some good riders up north."

"Well that may be, missy," Tim told her, "but what you call riders and what I call riders, I'll bet a hundred bucks are two different things." He twirled her again.

Josie just smiled. No use fighting a losing battle. The song ended, and she told Tim she did enjoy the dance; he told her it was his pleasure and escorted her back to her seat.

By this time Digger and Jaclyn were back at the table as well, bringing another round of longnecks over from the bar.

The singing, guitar and fiddle playing was the best Josie ever heard. The crowd loved it too, as they clapped loud and long after every song—for several hours. The night passed way too quickly; it was nearly midnight, and most of the crowd was gone except for a few diehards still there to hear the band's last few songs.

Josie happened to look over her left shoulder, to see the most handsome man she'd ever seen walk through the door. About 5'10", a blonde, well-built, athletic, toned and muscled man, with a sun-tanned face and professionally shaped Resistol cowboy hat, strolled over to the bar. As he walked away toward the bar, she noticed his Wranglers fit just right to show his good-looking butt and long legs. He wore black ostrich, handmade Lucchese cowboy boots, and a black ostrich belt with an older, big trophy belt buckle. His blue Cinch cowboy shirt was starched to perfection. He grabbed a Shiner Black Texas beer, took a big swig, and turned to look at the last of the crowd still in the bar.

She stopped breathing when she saw his eyes. She just stared. He was soooooo gorgeous. Those big eyes, bluer than sky blue, although with a tinge of sadness to them. She couldn't help but stare; he was the best-looking cowboy she'd ever seen. *Drop-dead gorgeous*, she thought *he could be a model or Western actor or someone famous.* He just kept sipping his beer, but couldn't help noticing the pretty little gal looking at him.

"Hey, Mr. Alan…come over here and sit down with us. Meet your new ranch hand!" Digger yelled.

Josie thought she'd die. That *is my boss???? Oh my God, he is so not what I pictured, not what I imagined, not, not…oh God, he's coming over here,* she said to herself.

"Hi, Digger and Jaclyn. You look lovely tonight, ma'am," he said to Jaclyn. "And what's this you're saying, Digger? We have a new ranch hand?" Alan inquired.

Digger pointed to Josie. "Yes, sir, this is Josie Lynn."

Josie made a nervous smile, "Hi," she shyly responded. "Pleased to meet you, sir."

"Well, they'll be no sir around here; please call me Alan," he said.

Josie nodded, still too shocked and staring at this attractive face looking at her.

"Who needs another beer?" Alan asked.

"Not me," said Digger. "Jaclyn's gotta get home."

Josie, who still had half a beer said, "That's okay, I'm ready when you guys are."

Alan said, "Well, I hate to drink alone, Josie. How 'bout we visit and finish our beers and I'll take you home…you're living at the ranch aren't you?"

"Oh, yes, sir—I mean Alan. I'm living at the ranch," Josie said, "but I don't want to bother you."

"It's no bother; besides, it will save Digger running you all the way back out to the ranch tonight," Alan insisted.

"Well, okay then, it's a deal," Josie told him.

Digger and Jaclyn left Hondo's and Josie and Alan worked on finishing those beers. Although she was worried about it being an awkward, uncomfortable situation, it never was. Josie and Alan talked and visited about Iowa, Texas, horses, Longhorn cattle, and Corgi dogs, until someone behind the bar yelled last call.

"Really?" Josie questioned, "We've been sitting here that long?"

"Guess so," said Alan. "You want another?"

"No, I've had plenty. Good to go," declared Josie.

"Sounds like a plan to me," replied Alan. Alan pulled her chair back as Josie got up from the table. She gave him a smile and out the door they went. There were still a few pickups on Main Street. Alan guessed they were at the new bar Crossroads, across the street from Hondo's.

They made their way to Alan's 2017 red Chevy Western Hauler one-ton truck. Even in the darkness, Josie could see all the chrome and fancy trim on the truck. Alan opened the door for Josie to get in, a gentleman's courtesy she wasn't used to. She thanked him, he walked around to his door, jumped in and away they went, heading back to the ranch.

"You're in the lookout seat," Alan informed her.

"Oooo-kay, what exactly does that mean, Alan?" Josie slowly said.

"That means when you see the deer standing on the shoulder of the road, tell me!" Alan said.

"Oh, sure, can do," Josie responded.

The curving, hilly ranch roads were more treacherous in the dark.

The turns came up fast and seemed sharper, the hills felt higher and the valleys felt steeper. It all went by so fast at night.

"Deer on the right!" Josie yelled.

Alan slowed down and veered left, narrowly missing a pack of 8 to 10 deer.

"Wait…that was a deer?" Josie inquired.

"Yeah, you called it," Alan responded.

"But they're so little…" Josie answered, "not much bigger than greyhound dogs."

"Well, you're used to those big corn-fed deer up in Iowa. Texas deer are much smaller. But they come out to the edge of the roads at night to eat the best grass, that's why so many of us run with guards on front of our trucks, to protect the front end from deer, and cows that might push on a truck when we're driving through the pastures."

"I see," Josie pondered. "Hope we don't see any more tonight."

They made their way on Old San Antonio Road to the ranch driveway, and turned up the private road. They saw numerous deer out in the pastures grazing with the horses as the truck headlights shined on them as they rounded the curves of the ranch drive.

"Looks like your herd increases at night," Josie giggled.

"Yeah, guess so. I don't mind. Kinda fun to sit on the porch and watch all the deer around here," Alan commented.

"Oh, I suppose so," Josie said.

They wound up the road, turning in toward the barns and the cabin. "Here's your stop," Alan declared.

"Thank you so much, Mr. Sutcliff…uhhh, Alan. Appreciate the ride home, and the good company," Josie expressed.

"My pleasure," Alan said with a big smile as he tipped his hat to her.

Josie went to the cabin, and once inside she leaned back on the closed door. Maverick came to greet her. "Wow," she said to herself, "what am I in for? The kindest, best looking man I've ever met is married….oh well. I'm not looking for *any* more relationships, anyway. Such a shame though. He's a keeper."

She kicked off her boots, pulled off her jeans and shirt, and fell into bed. The Corgi jumped in bed too, and gave her a big lick on the face. She pulled up the covers, and they were both snoring within minutes.

Chapter 6

After dropping off Josie at the cabin, Alan turned back on the road toward the ranch house. Driving past Steve and Bob's houses, he pulled into the ranch house circle drive, shut off the engine and went into the house. The lights were off and he didn't find Nikky anywhere. Seemed odd to him. No note on the kitchen counter to let him know just where she was. Even more odd, her Escalade was in the garage. *Could she just be out with friends?* He didn't think so, but that must be the explanation. He checked his cell phone—no missed calls. *Guess she doesn't much give a shit if she lets me know where she's at,* he summarized.

He was not surprised. Things hadn't been good between them for months, maybe years. He reflected back on their marriage. She seemed happy, he thought. He needed a companion to share life with, as though that was something missing from his life. His friends convinced him of it.

But she wasn't happy. He'd bought her everything, taken her on trips, done everything he could to ensure her happiness, thinking that if she was happy he could go along in life convincing himself that he was happy. He didn't love her, but he thought he could live with her, and he persuaded himself to believe marriage was a good thing.

It wasn't working. She was miserable, almost acting like she hated him most of the time. She would snap at him in a wickedly sarcastic voice, belittle him in front of friends, and challenge him in front of the barn help. Tormented was what he felt most of the time, wondering what had he gotten himself into. Why couldn't he have found a genuinely happy girl who just wanted to share life and love with him? His sex life was non-existent with Nikky. Hadn't made love in months. Maybe over a year. He couldn't even remember. She always had an excuse. Finally, he just got tired of trying. He wasn't the type of man to give up on something or someone, but Nikky had defeated him. Depressed him. Made him feel like retreating at the house to just pass time. And that's what he did. Day after day.

Not sure why he'd gotten the wild hair to go to town tonight. Something just told him to go. He liked supporting the local businesses, he liked the gals running Hondo's. He was glad he stopped in there and got to see Digger, Jaclyn and Josie. They were five to ten years younger than he, but being around them made him feel alive.

He filled a glass with ice in the dark kitchen, grabbed a bottle and walked out the sliding patio door to sit on the large rustic wooden porch with a nightcap of Crown Royal. A sipper is what he needed. No lights on, he just relaxed in the quiet wilderness in a comfy chair on the porch, listening to the sounds of the night.

He could see the lights of many hills in the distance, other ranches and small communities' lights. It was peaceful. He heard a horse whinny. He sipped the Crown. It was a beautiful starry night. The Texas moon, half full, stretched white like a smile.

He was half asleep when he heard rustling in the nearby grass and bush. He sat quiet. He stopped breathing just to strain his hearing to make out the source of the noises. It was whispering….whispering, and soft muffled giggling that he heard. He sat quiet, straining to determine whose voices he was hearing.

Then total silence for what seemed like an hour, but probably was only a minute or two. Followed by low deep groans, and kissing noises. No talking—he heard lips smacking together. He sat motionless at the far end of the porch. More kissing. More moaning. Finally, he heard whispers.

"I gotta go. I'll come to the barn tomorrow." The voice was Nikky's. Even muffled and whispered, Alan knew it was her.

Another whispered voice followed… "Come on down, baby, I'll show you what a real stud horse can do." Muffled giggles and more kissing sounds invaded the night.

Alan could not believe what he was hearing. Had he had too much to drink? Was he imagining all this? Trying to control himself from leaping out of the chair and confronting whoever it was, he remained quiet and still. The sound of a door opening, then closing. More rustling in the grass and bushes. They're gone.

He pondered for hours what he'd just witnessed, trying to absorb it all. So, Nikky's been unfaithful and messing with someone; the only logical answer is Steve.

Alan sat up most of the night in the porch chair, his body frozen in a range of emotions as big as the Texas sky. He struggled with suspicion, disbelief, betrayal, anger, pain and sadness. He was unable to move and unable to sleep. He sipped the Crown until most of the bottle was gone and the morning sun was coming up.

Chapter 7

Day broke in the Hill Country. Alan heard horses in the barn whinnying to be fed. He was sure the Mexicans were there doing chores; Bob was probably down there, too. Alan had one hell of a headache, but that pain was nowhere near the pain he felt in his heart. He'd been betrayed.

Still in the same clothes from the night before, he got in his golf cart to drive down to the show barn. He looked like hell. Bob saw him first, knowing full well something was going on—something not so good. Alan pulled up and shut off the golf cart. Bob offered him a cigarette. "Do I look that bad?" Alan asked. Bob just kept staring at Alan, holding out the pack of cigarettes.

"Let's go in the office; I need to talk," Alan demanded, as he held the office door open for Bob. Two hours went by; the men walked out of the office.

By this time, all the ranch hands except Steve are in the barn, doing various chores necessary for running a productive horse ranch. Josie caught a glimpse of Alan as he headed for the golf cart. She wondered why in the world he was still in the same clothes as last night.

Around 11:00, Bob called Josie, Digger, Chico and Pedro into his office. He said he's got some odd jobs that have been needing to get done, and today was the day to do them. He sent the Mexicans in the gator to fix fence at the west end of the ranch, a 30-minute gator ride away. He told Josie and Digger they needed to sort colts in the yearling pen and pick out the best four to start for show prep. There were several big pens out in the pasture to push the colts into, then sort off the ones to hold back, and run them up the lane to keep them in a separate pen

35

south of the mare motel. Everyone had their jobs that should take most of the day. Digger and Josie left on another gator to head for the yearling pasture.

Steve had made his way to the barn by this time. "Where the hell is everybody?" Steve asked.

"Got 'em all out doing jobs that'll take most of the day," Bob replied. "No riding today. Gotta spend a day getting other shit done. I'm delivering a broodmare to the Bar S Ranch near Houston. Got the place to yourself, Stevie," Bob said as he walked out the alleyway to load the trailer with a broodmare and baby.

"Well, that's interesting," Steve said. "I got the place to myself… don't mind if I do!" Steve grabbed his cell phone and made a call. Half an hour later, Nikky showed up at the barn.

"Are you serious? Everyone's gone?" Nikky asked.

"Yup, it's true,'" Steve said as he leaned in for a kiss. Then lips together, he backed Nikky up to the door, pressing her into the closed door, rubbing hard against her.

"Let's go in the office," she whispered.

Once in the office, Nikky locked the doors and pulled the window blinds shut. The barn radio in the alley was playing country music; the barn was relatively quiet. There was no one around. Steve coaxed Nikky to take her top off.

"What if someone comes in?" she asked.

"Nobody is anywhere around here," Steve answered, while kissing her soft lips. With her back against the wall, and topless, she quickly unbuttoned Steve's shirt.

"Our plan is going along well, isn't it, Stevie?" Nikky asked.

"Yes, we get all the horses we want with Alan's checkbook, paying huge inflated prices, then the sellers give us a 50% commission payback."

"What could be better?" Nikky said with a giggle.

"Less fabric between us would be better," Steve replied. Nikky grinned and unzipped her jeans first, then his. The jeans fall to their ankles. Deep in passionate kisses and totally consumed with each other, Steve and Nikky dropped more clothes, until both are completely naked and embraced.

BANG! BANG! Nikky screamed! Gun blasts had just blown the

handle off the office door. *BANG!* The door was kicked wide open and Alan stood in the doorway, holding a .357 Magnum handgun pointed directly toward Steve and Nikky.

"Well, good morning to you both," Alan announced calmly.

Nikky was shaking and crying, Steve grabbing for his clothes that were strewn all over the floor.

"It seems that you two worthless pieces of shit have 15 minutes to find another place to live," Alan sternly informed them.

"What?" cried Nikky. "What are you talking about, Alan? I love you!"

"Yeah, love me like a rattlesnake…14 minutes and counting," Alan replied.

"Can I get my paycheck?" Steve asked.

"No, you sorry son of a bitch, but you can get the hell outta here!" Alan yelled impatiently. *"Both of you*…13 minutes!"

Steve grabbed his clothes and ran for his pickup, Nikky close behind.

"You'll come to your senses, Alan. I'll be at the Inn at Barons Creek in town waiting for you to come talk," Nikky pled on her way out.

"Don't bet on it, bitch," Alan replied in a deep, disgusted tone.

Steve and Nikky drove up to the houses on the hill, grabbed what belongings fit into four suitcases, and left the ranch.

Hearing the gunshots, Josie and Digger came flying up the pasture lane to the show barn.

"What the hell is going on in here?" Digger yelled through the barn.

No answer.

Digger and Josie ran up the barn alley toward the office. Hearing his running bootsteps and spurs jingling, horses started spinning and bucking in their stalls, getting all excited. Digger made his way to the office with Josie close on his heels. Alan was sitting in the large leather office chair, kicked back with his boots on the desktop, looking out the window. The .357 was laying on the desk. Digger and Josie stopped in horror, wondering what in the world just took place here.

"Don't see no blood, Mr. Alan…everything okay in here?" Digger asked, out of breath.

"Oh yeah," replies Alan in a whimsical tone. "I was just doing a little rattlesnake hunting." Josie and Digger looked at each other, thinking, *What in the hell is he talking about?*

"You got any beer hid in this barn, Digger?" Alan asked.

"Well, yeah," replied Digger. He made his way to the secret refrigerator in the tack room, grabbed three Lone Stars, and rushed back to the office. Josie remained frozen in place until Digger bumped her in the arm to take a beer. She looked at Digger, wide-eyed and very puzzled.

"There are gonna be some major changes around here starting today," Alan advised, opening and sipping an ice-cold longneck.

Still dumbfounded, Josie and Digger take big gulps from their beers.

"Ooo-kay," Digger slowly spoke.

"I'll be running the ranch again, making the decisions, working out here with you all," Alan began. "We're gonna be selling off those studs and a lot of these damn show horses. We're gonna make this ranch a working cow horse training facility. And *Digger,*" Alan continued, "you're officially the new head trainer." Digger's mouth dropped wide open.

Just then, Bob walked into the office.

"Get all the evidence you needed, Boss?" Bob wondered.

"Sure did, Bob. Digger, run get Bob a beer, would ya please?"

"Sure thing, Boss," Digger replied.

Josie was downing that beer like it was 120 degrees and she was dying of thirst. She couldn't believe the events of this day. But she was relieved—relieved that Alan was finally free from the wicked witch of a wife. Although she was not sure what all went on in this office, it was easy to see Alan was liberated. He was not going to be miserable anymore. He was in control now, and his confidence was evident. Alan was glad to be alive today. Glad the turn of events was done. Glad to be rid of the two-timing, poor excuse-of-a-wife he had, and the no-good horse trainer—both had ripped him off for hundreds of thousands of dollars.

But unbeknown to all, Alan had declared privately to himself never to get married again.

Chapter 8

The next few months were much happier for everyone on the ranch. Alan had secretly taped the conversation between Steve and Nikky to have evidence for a lawsuit, should either one of them contest Steve's firing or Alan and Nikky's impending divorce. Alan had cancelled all Nikky's credit cards, taken her name off every account they had together before coming to the barn to confront them both with the gun. They had signed a prenuptial so he wasn't worried about her financial gains on anything he owned. He never intended to shoot anyone that day, but he knew he had to take aggressive action to get rid of those two.

And with the burden lifted off him, although Alan was empty and sad about a failed marriage that he knew wasn't right from the start, it was in his best interest that things turned out the way that they did. He focused on the future for inner strength. Looking *forward*, he decided, was much better for the soul than looking back!

Bob had been in with Alan on the setup plan to catch Steve and Nikky in the barn that day. Bob was as surprised as Alan that something was going on with the two, but remained loyal to his boss in coordinating a plan to find out the truth.

Digger had taken over all the training, moved into Steve's ranch house on the hill, provided by Alan as part of the pay for the head trainer. Together, Digger and Bob had sold the two stallions, most of the high dollar halter horses, seven of the pleasure horses and thirty head of broodmares, with the best thirty remaining. Still plenty of horses left for Digger to train on—there were all the two year olds to start breaking and training, yearlings to break to lead and lunge, and babies to halter break.

There was one pleasure mare, the dun, that was still at the ranch.

Bob had seen what a liking Josie had taken to that mare. Because of the abuse Steve had given to the dun, Bob had turned the mare out in a big pasture with old Bozo, just to have some time off and forget about the bad training sessions Steve had given her. This would give her time to just be a horse again.

Josie was happy as ever. It was pure fun working in the barn. She groomed the two year olds, carefully and slowly saddling them before Digger would take them out to lunge and ride. You never knew what to expect with the colts. Some were gentle and willing but a little scared as the big saddle was placed up on their back. Others would jump and flinch for weeks just being brushed, and they took longer to saddle the first time. But it was all worth it. These were smart, well-bred two year olds, with quiet "cat like" movement and cadence as they seemed to float around the arena under saddle.

There were some great colts in the bunch. Some high-dollar selling colts, maybe even some futurity winners. Futurity shows were specifically for young horses to be in competition together. Josie was excited to be a part of it all. It was rewarding to take a colt from the gawky know-nothing stage and making him into a beautiful, confident horse that obeyed the rider's every cue.

Alan was an active part of the horse business now, too. At the barn every day, he did the records and bookkeeping end of the business on the computer in the office, watched and encouraged Digger riding the colts, checked fence and pastures on the gator, and would secretly watch Josie through the office window as she brushed, washed and loved on the young colts and fillies. He thought she was amazing. He'd never seen a woman so fulfilled with what she was doing, so willing to be part of a team. Grooming horses, she recognized, was a vital step toward training and sales and profit for the ranch. He could see how dedicated she was, working long days, sometimes into the evening just to make sure the barns and horses were up to her standards of perfection. He learned by watching her that she took great pride in the ranch, nearly as much as he did. He loved to just watch her.

Josie had a spring in her step as she reached the barn door, her Corgi dog close behind, both enjoying the 75-degree sunny morning. Digger arrived at the barn door at nearly the same time.

"What you looking so happy about, Miss Josie?" he asked.

"It's my birthday, and I'm just happy," was her quick reply.

"Oh, well then, Happy Birthday…why didn't you let me know? I'd have baked a cake!" Digger bantered.

"Pfffffttt" Josie replied, "don't need no cake, just buy me a beer!"

"Okay, that works!" Digger declared as they walked down the concrete alleyway in the show barn.

The smell was delightful, fresh alfalfa hay and sweet molasses feed filled Josie's nose as she and Maverick went down the alley, checking every stall to see that all the horses were enjoying breakfast. She headed for the big coffee pot in the office. Digger was already there, as were Alan and Bob.

"Josie's birthday today," announced Digger. "Maybe she needs a spanking," he chuckled.

"You do and you'll end up with your boots in the water tank, cowboy!" Josie replied sternly.

"Happy birthday to you, Josie!" both Bob and Alan exclaimed in unison.

"Any special plans for the day?" Alan asked.

"Hummm, not really," said Josie "just another day here in paradise."

Alan smiled. "Josie, do you ride?" he asked.

"Ride?" Josie questioned.

"Yeah, you know, in a saddle, feet in the stirrups, horse moving under you…shit like that…RIDE!" said Alan.

"Well, yes, sir, I do," stated Josie. "Haven't for a long time, but I can ride."

Alan looked at Bob, "What about bringing up the dun mare from the lower pasture?" he asked.

"Sure thing, Boss, I'll send Pedro. . .Fredro. . .Saidrow, or whatever his name is, out to fetch her."

Alan looked deep into Josie's flashing eyes. "Happy birthday," he whispered.

"Ohhhhhh, you're bringing her in for me to ride? How awesome!" Josie giggled and wiggled with delight.

"No," replied Alan in a quiet tone, "I'm giving her to you."

"What? Giving her to me?" Josie shouted. "You're gonna do *that?"*

"I can do whatever I want, Miss Josie, and I want you to have her for a birthday present!" Alan declared.

"Oh, *my God!*" Josie squealed as she did salsa dance steps right there in the office, the men just laughing at her. Bob muttered something under his laugh about her hanging around those damn Mexicans too much.

Josie stopped in her tracks and looked at Alan. "How can I ever thank you enough?"

"Just keep enjoying life and this ranch like I've seen you do the last three months. That and a simple thank you will do," Alan replied. Josie did the salsa dance some more, this time dancing her way right out of the office and down the barn paved alleyway. Maverick was barking constantly and loud, and jumping up beside her, he so excited seeing her dancing in the horse barn it got him all revved up. She had the biggest smile on her face as she danced by herself nearly ten minutes. The men in the office just chuckling at seeing such a crazy, happy woman, and what a good thing it was.

Fifteen minutes passed very slowly for Josie, who was polishing saddles and cleaning up the tack room; finally she heard clip clop, clip clop, clip clop. The dun mare was being led in the barn by Pancho the Mexican. He was leading the dun in one hand and Bozo the chestnut gelding in the other. They looked a little rough and the sun had faded their hair coat color, but Josie knew that was cosmetic and she could put that winning-glow hair coat back on in no time. She eagerly took the dun mare from Pancho and put her in the crossties, two big chains hanging from the top of opposite stall fronts, with snaps on the end that snapped to either side of the halter. In the crossties, Josie could navigate fully around the mare without having to move her.

"She is just as gorgeous as I remember," Josie said.

"*Sí*, good looking mare," was Pancho's response, nodding his head.

Chapter 9

Josie groomed and brushed the mare, talking in a soft, calm voice and just brushing and touching her with gentle hands all over her body. The mare stood quietly in the crossties, her big soft brown eyes watching and sensing Josie's every move. She smelled like horse, a distinct smell only a cowgirl loves. Her hair coat was soft, although faded from sun damage. Josie brushed out dirt, and loose, dead hair off the mare, until there was a good sized pile on the floor under her.

"Ready to saddle up?" Alan asked as he walked from the office to the barn alley.

"Yup, I'm ready" Josie replied.

"Care if I ride with you?" Alan asked.

"That'd be awesome!" Josie exclaimed. "Don't think I've ever seen you ride."

"Well that makes two of us, 'cause I've never seen you ride," he said.

They both stirred up a nervous chuckle. Alan moved Bozo from the wash rack, back to another set of crossties and grabbed a brush to clean him up. Josie finished work on the dun mare, now named Hope. *Hope* was the word that summarized what Josie felt now. Where she once was destitute, lonely, and down on life and love, now she had hope....and "Hope" had her.

Josie and Alan met at the same time in the tack room to get saddles. Josie brushed past Alan, reaching for the Jeff Smith training saddle. Alan catches a whiff of Josie's sweet perfume, and felt a warm tingle inside, as he stood beside her preparing to lift the Martin saddle off the rack.

They both stopped, looked at each other, and Josie, with big tears in her eyes and lump in her throat, mustered a, "Thank you, Alan," in a cracked voice.

Alan stopped reaching for the saddle, turned toward Josie and hugged her tightly. Oh, his arms had ached to hold her, her hair smelled so good, so fresh; the embrace felt even more wonderful as Alan felt Josie hugging him tightly back.

"What took you so long?" Josie whispered still locked tight in the embrace.

"What took *you* so long?" Alan whispered back, as he gave her a kiss on the cheek. He reached for his handkerchief in his back pocket and gave it to her.

She's a bit embarrassed by the tears, but took it and wiped her eyes, then looked at him with a big grin.

"Let's ride!" Josie shouted. He smiled and nodded.

They both saddled up, and led the horses to the arena to lunge. Josie figured the mare may have a bit of buck in her, not being ridden for so long; it was best to find out when she was standing on the ground, rather than sitting in the saddle. She sent the mare out on the line and sure enough, that mare gave three good bucks, then settled down to a smooth-gaited canter, barely touching the ground with her soft movement. Alan sent Bozo out on a lunge line too, the old horse snorted and kicked up his heels like a young colt. After three rounds of fast bucking and running, Bozo slowed to a trot, not even wanting to go fast anymore. He was ready to ride. So were Hope and Josie. They both took the halters off and put bridles on, then both riders prepared to mount up. Alan stood by Bozo, just watching Josie.

Josie stepped in the stirrup, glanced back at Alan, saying, "What are you doing?"

"Just enjoying the view," was Alan's response. Josie shook her head sideways. Alan stepped up and swung into Bozo's saddle and both made a few rounds in the arena, walking at first, then a trot, then finally a lope.

Josie couldn't believe how good a rider Alan was. Alan was thinking the same thing about Josie. Heels deep in the stirrup, shoulders back, hands soft and low, both riders showed experience and confidence as they controlled the speed and movement of their horses. Josie was impressed watching Alan. *This guy's a pro*, she thought.

Alan said, "Why the heck haven't you been riding here before now, cowgirl? You're a great hand with a horse."

"Well," Josie started, "number one, nobody asked me to, and number two, you Texans don't think Yankees can ride a lick."

Alan snorted and snickered. "Guess that'll change on both accounts!"

Digger stepped into the arena to watch both of them ride and said, "Well, gollllyyyy! Look at you two. What a perfect pair!" Josie grinned and just kept loping the mare in circles.

Alan pulled Bozo up to a stop, then backed him and said, "Let's get outta here, Jos." She nodded and out of the arena they went toward the pasture.

"Hope is fabulous, Alan," Josie declared.

"Hope? "Alan wondered.

"Yeah, this mare—I named her Hope," replied Josie.

"Ohhhh, why?" Alan questioned her.

"Because hope is just what I'm feeling. I could have named her Happy, but that sounds too stupid" Josie said.

Alan agreed with a chuckle.

"And," Josie continued, "she just looks like Hope."

"Well, Hope it is," said Alan. They rode down the pasture lane at a soft jog trot, both horses ears up, looking straight ahead, occasional switch of the tail to hit a fly. The horses were as content as the riders.

Making their way to a big gate, Alan opened and closed the gate on horseback, doing a maneuver of side steps by the horse from leg cues given by the rider, and the pair resumed the jog trot up and over a big grass hill. As they got to the top of the hill, Josie pulled back on the reins to bring Hope to a quick stop.

"Whoa," Josie said. "Look at all the beautiful blue flowers!"

"They're Texas bluebonnets, very common in Hill Country," Alan replied, looking at the thick, brilliant lavender-blue flowers entirely covering the hillside, swaying in the breeze. Josie just had to stop and absorb all the beauty that lay in front of her. They both took deep breaths and admired the scenery. Life was good.

They rode along the edge of the bluebonnet field heading up a trail toward a steep, jagged mountain ridge. As they got closer to the ridge, Josie saw sharp granite rocks, small cactus and mesquite, cedar and scrub evergreen trees, growing everywhere. The further on the trail they went, the more dense the trees and cactus got, but the smell was wonderful. The combination of evergreen and cedar was a deep, powerful smell. A rabbit scurried across the trail. Hope stopped to stare at it, but doesn't spook it; she then continued walking with a gentle heel nudge from Josie. Hope led the way on the narrow cowpath trail, Bozo walked calmly, half asleep, following closely behind Hope's tail. Josie and Alan rode relaxed in their saddles as they climbed up the red dirt trail, winding around the huge granite boulder that loomed just to their right. Finally, they came to a clearing, a large patch of grass with a granite boulder nearby to sit on.

"How 'bout a break?" Josie asked.

"Sure," Alan replied, "been awhile since my butt sat in a saddle this long." They dismounted, slowly, feeling some potentially sore muscles as they stepped down, finally on the ground. They each took a rein and tied their horses to a nearby tree.

Josie was rubbing her butt and legs with her hands, and she could feel the sore stiffness that sets in when a rider's not in shape.

"Need some help with that?" Alan asks. Josie gave him a grin and rolled her eyes while shaking her head in a "whatever" kind of way. Josie headed for the rock, climbed up on it just to get a better view of the valley below. Alan was right behind her. She stopped on the rock, just looking at the panoramic view.

"It's breathtaking," Josie said. "You can see for miles and miles. The tree tops, the hills of all different shapes and sizes. Some with flat tops, some with rounded hill tops where only cactus grows, and yet others with jagged rough rocks covering the hills. Why is there a blue haze off in the distant hills?" Josie inquired as she felt Alan lean into her, right behind her pressing against her body.

"Well, there are so many cedar trees," he says in a soft voice, "that's actually cedar pollen you're seeing that's given off by the trees." He slipped his arms around her waist and locked his wrists together. Josie leaned back against him.

"It's just amazing here, like Texas' best kept secret," Josie said.

He put his face up to her hair and ear and softly said, "And we need to keep it that way; don't be telling anyone how beautiful our Texas Hill Country is; they'll all want to live here."

Josie smiled, content in the embrace for several minutes, just enjoying the beauty of the Hill Country, the closeness of each other. Alan spun Josie around to face him, delicately touched the side of her chin, tipped his head slightly and kissed her soft lips. As the moment progressed, Josie melted into the kiss. She felt the passion, the physical strength and sexual desire of this man.

The kiss ended, they pulled back slightly, but stared intently, into each other's eyes. *I've made so many mistakes before,* Josie told herself, *but this time it will be different. It just* has *to be different.* She reassured herself this was like no other man she'd ever met. This was the one. She tipped her head, allowing it to miss the brim of his cowboy hat, and she kissed him with all the love she'd held inside her for years with a never-ending, sensual, deep kiss.

The kiss was followed with several more little, soft kisses. Alan wrapped his arms totally around Josie and hugged her.

"How about some birthday supper?" Alan asked.

Realizing she'd hardly eaten anything today, Josie replied with a big smile and nod. Alan untied Hope's rein from the tree and handed it to Josie; at the same time, Josie was untying Bozo from a tree and handed the reins to Alan. They both smiled at each other, and prepared to mount. After they were mounted, they made their way back down the narrow trail through the pasture, past the bluebonnet flowers, and back to the ranch lane up to the barn.

Digger and Bob were sweeping up the alleyway in the barn as Josie and Alan stopped and got off outside the barn and led their horses in.

"Looks like someone's having a pretty good birthday," Digger said.

Josie gave a big grin and thumbs up back to him.

"I'm gonna rinse these two off," Josie let everyone know. She led Hope into the wash rack, unsaddled and started bathing the mare. After a quick soaping, rinsing and wiping with the scraper to remove excess water, she sprayed her down with hair coat conditioner then backed her out of the wash rack and put Hope in a stall. Josie did the same routine with Bozo, as Alan watched her while sitting on a bucket turned upside down just across the alleyway.

After Bozo was bathed, Josie put him in a fresh bedded stall next to Hope. These stalls did have two-year-olds in them this morning, but Bob and Digger's intuition must have told them to have them ready for Hope and Bozo.

"Be cleaned up and ready in an hour?" Alan asked Josie.

"Sure thing!" she quickly responded.

"I'll be down to pick ya up then," Alan says with a wink at Josie, he left the barn.

"If I'm dreaming, I don't *ever* want to wake up!" Josie whispered to herself.

Chapter 10

Josie ran all the way to the cabin, the Corgi close behind. She opened the cabin door and to her total surprise, a dozen long-stemmed red roses in a hand-painted vase were sitting on her kitchen island. The vase was as beautiful as the roses—intricate, hand-painted details of wild horses running free over the hills, probably created by one of the many local artists. The strong, wonderful smell of roses filled the entire cabin. *Alan?* Josie wondered. How did he get those roses in here without her seeing him?

She could only spend a few minutes admiring and smelling the sweet rose scent. She hit the message button on the answering machine to listen to birthday wishes from both Sierra and Marne. Wow, it had been a long time since she talked to them. She had emailed a few times, sending photos of the ranch and Hill Country. She had never let them know her true feelings for Alan, or all the episodes from the ranch. It was nice to get the greeting from her friends; she'd have to call them back personally, but not tonight. She glanced at the clock, and kicked into high gear—a quick shower, fast application of make-up and mascara. She threw on clean, tight jeans, a fitted, soft-knit top with colored rhinestones and pictures of bucking horses. She pulled on comfy Justin boots and bling—a glitzy studded cowboy belt. A touch of spray in her long, naturally wavy hair that feathered down her neck and onto her shoulders.

Josie heard a truck pull up in front of the cabin as she kissed her dog on the head, and ran toward the door. She heard knock-knock-knock on the front door. *This guy really is a gentleman*, she thought. She opened the door to find Alan looking like a million bucks. Starched Cinch jeans with a navy blue shirt, his Loveless, custom-made cowboy boots and belt with the silver trophy buckle displayed his professional cowboy look. Adding his George Strait black felt hat with a square shaped front brim accentuated his great look.

"My, you look fine tonight, sir," Josie exclaimed.

"Well, thank you, ma'am. I'm saying the same about you." He leaned in to give her a kiss on the cheek.

"I sure had a nice surprise when I got in here a bit ago." Josie mentioned the beautiful red roses in a hand painted vase.

Alan smiled, his brilliant blue eyes sparkling as he gazed into her endless brown eyes.

"Thank you, Mr. Wonderful," Josie whispered softly.

"You're very welcome, Ms. Amazing!" Alan quipped back. "Are ya hungry for brisket and peach cobbler, a real Texas Hill Country treat?" Alan asked.

"Sure am!" Josie said with a big grin. She grabbed his hand and they walked out hand-in-hand to the truck.

Heading down Old San Antonio ranch road to highway 290 west, through Fredericksburg, then north on highway 16 toward Llano—a forty-minute drive, reminiscing about the happiest-day-ever today, they ended up at Cooper's Barbeque.

"Ever been here, Josie?" Alan asked.

"Nope, sure haven't. I'm pretty content to stay on the ranch in my cabin and just enjoy life," Josie answered.

"Well, let's see if ya like this joint. You Iowans do know what good barbeque is, don't cha?" Alan asked.

Josie gave a big grin.

Upon arriving, he escorted her up to the massive barbeque pits. The incredible barbeque smell nearly made her drool. A young man lifted the big pit lid to show the selection available.

"Oh, my gosh." Josie had never seen such a good looking selection of meat. "What is all this?" she asked.

The young man tending the pit gave her a grin and using his long barbeque fork he pointed to each item, explaining. "This is pork ribs, here's beef ribs, here's turkey, here's half a chicken, here's sausage, here's sausage with jalapeno, here's pork loin and here's our famous brisket." He pointed to a huge hunk of meat nearly black on top, but red brown inside.

"Ohhhh, what a decision!" she said, glancing a worried look at Alan. "Help me!" she said.

Alan spoke up, "We'll take a pound of brisket."

The young man sliced off a hunk, then dipped it in a huge steel pot of special-recipe barbeque sauce. He grabbed a tray and a piece of freezer paper and tossed the brisket on it, handing it to Alan. Alan took the tray of meat and they walked into the restaurant.

The smell inside was enticing, too, Josie noticed as she walked by the case containing hot peach and blueberry cobblers.

"We need some peach cobbler, please, sir," Alan told the man behind the counter.

"Yes, sir!" The man quickly grabbed a big spoon and dished up a huge portion of peach cobbler into a Styrofoam bowl. Moving down the line in front of the counter, Alan grabbed two Lone Star longnecks and asks Josie if she wanted any salads.

"Oh, my, no, I think we've got plenty right here," was her answer as Alan paid the cashier.

Alan directed Josie to hold the beers and follow him. They made their way to the bean pot, a huge, hot kettle full of pinto beans and sauce. There was another huge pot, full to the top of barbeque sauce. And yet another giant bowl of fresh cut chunks of onion. Alan used the dipper and filled bowls with all three fixings. Making their way to the picnic tables, they grabbed silverware and white freezer paper.

Sitting down and opening the beers, Josie watched as Alan prepared the brisket. Opening the pink paper the brisket was wrapped in, he put the white glossy paper in front of her and pushed several big pieces of brisket off onto the paper.

"Dig in!" he commanded.

Seemed pretty strange, eating off paper, but Josie just assumed this was Texas custom, and grabbed her fork to get that first bite.

"Ooohhhhhh, myyyyyy!" Josie declared. "How do they make this sooooooo good?" She savored another bite, holding it in her mouth just to get all the succulent flavors in her palate. "How in the world is it sweet, peppery, and salty all at once?" she asked.

"It's the rub," replied Alan. "The rub is the seasonings they put on the meat before it's slow-cooked ten to twelve hours in a pit over mesquite wood."

"Well, that explains *why* it's so damn good!" Josie said, as she took another bite that seemed to melt in her mouth. "Oh, my word, I've died and gone to heaven…this is best piece of meat I've ever had!" Josie declared.

Alan smiled. "This place is world famous; guess they ship it all over the country."

"I can taste why," Josie said with a big grin.

They finished the delicious, moist brisket while enjoying the beer, and Alan leaned into her and whispered, "Best is for last."

"The cobbler?" Josie wondered.

Alan pushed the bowl of steamy hot cobbler towards her—loaded with big peaches, sauce and soft chunks of cobbler breading. She tried a bite.

She shut her eyes and said, "Mmmmm….this is incredible!"

Alan smiled and grabbed a fork to dig in himself. The ate every bite slowly, then licked their forks until every drop of peach cobbler was gone.

"What a treat!" Josie declared "What a treat! They just don't make brisket and peach cobbler this good up in Iowa!"

Alan gave a sly smile. "You are in Texas, little lady. Everything is bigger and better in Texas. Guess we better go dance off some of this supper now," Alan said.

"Another great plan," Josie said as she seconded that thought.

Near dusk, they left Llano, drove back down highway 16 through Fredericksburg and kept going.

"Not stopping at Hondo's?" Josie asked.

"Not tonight; got something else in mind," Alan replied as he drove to the flashing light four miles east of town, turned right and headed south.

They arrived at their destination. In the dark, Josie could see a big parking lot near two old vintage buildings, one large and one smaller.

"This is Luckenbach?" Josie asked.

"It sure is. Welcome to Luckenbach," Alan answered.

Josie couldn't quite believe her eyes. She noticed a big old-fashioned dance hall made of weathered barn boards, with big side openings propped open with a board. There was a smaller building of similar vintage construction with a post office sign hanging over the front door. They went inside that building, to find a small general store full of tee shirts, caps, coffee cups and sale items. Further back through the little store she could hear country music songs being sung and guitars playing.

They went through the store to the bar. *So* this *is Luckenbach,* Josie thought to herself. *How interesting.* The bar was a small room, about twenty by twenty feet with a large L-shaped bar across two of the four walls. A big wood-burning stove sat in the middle of the floor. There were three benches and two stools along the wall and in front of the bar. In the corner was a small table with four cowboys and one cowgirl sitting on old metal chairs singing sweet country tunes and playing guitars and fiddles. Now this is Luckenbach, Josie thought. There was a crowd of 18 people sitting and standing, drinking beer, tapping toes and loving the good old country music these folks were offering for all to enjoy. Original songs or well-known songs, the group sang them all to the small crowd's delight.

Alan made his way to the bar to get two cold beers. Folks were polite to move out of the way; it was so crowded, but they sure let him get to the bar to get the beer. Josie found spots on a bench along the bar for them to sit.

It took her a few minutes to realize just what was going on. As the band talked and visited in between songs, she figured out that they weren't a real band, but rather a circle of friends or "pickers," as they're known. Whenever anyone had extra time they stopped in to Luckenbach just to play and grin and get together. One fella would start the song, the others watched just a bit, then jumped in, playing their guitars or violins, and instantly it was a beautiful, harmonized tune. Their voices and instruments blended perfectly. Another pleasant surprise was when the bartender started playing harmonica from behind the bar. It was amazing, goose-bump moments for Josie to hear all these folks playing so well and sounding so good together. It was Texas tradition, and everyone was loving it. Josie hoped this night would never end.

As she sat she took in all the sights of this little cozy cabin with a bar. The open ceiling had wooden rafters that were covered by caps and cowboy boots and cowboy hats that were hanging up there. Everything up there was filthy, must have been three layers of dirt on them since they'd been there a long, long time. All the walls were plastered with bumper stickers, posters, pictures of Hondo, photographs of Jerry Jeff Walker, Willie Nelson and more. There was a big moose or cow or some kind of stuffed head hanging over the bar with a wooden sign on it. The handwriting under the animal head said, "Luckenbach Squirrel." There was a big oil painting of Hondo over the bar. There was a giant Lone Star Beer sign shot full of bullet holes hanging on one wall near the ceiling.

"Well, the place sure has character," Josie said to Alan.

"Lots of history, and *lots* of music, too" Alan add. "If these walls could talk . . ." he wondered. They sipped the cold beers, and enjoyed the surroundings.

Sometime later, the pickers quit playing, but announced to the crowd that the dance was starting in the dance hall in five minutes. The crowd applauded; many folks put dollars in the tip jar on the small table, and made their way over to the hall.

Alan and Josie grabbed two more Lone Stars and strolled across the street to the dance hall where the "Almost Patsy Cline Band" was about to play. Hearing the first verse, Josie knew she'd love this band. Great tunes, sung with incredibly good voices—the dance floor quickly fills up with cowboys and cowgirls doing the Texas two-step.

"Gotta go!" declared Alan. And off they went, to dance the night away enjoying each other's company with tighter embraces each dance.

The music ended after four wonderful hours of songs and guitars and dancing. Alan and Josie called it a night and headed back to the ranch.

Leaving Luckenbach, the winding ranch roads were full of critters. Dead armadillos and racoons lay along the road. Live critters ran across the road. Alan took it slow to miss the deer and skunks.

As they reached one high hilltop, Josie gasped, "That's the most beautiful sight ever!" as she looked over the Hill Country toward the town that was full of lights.

"It is a real pretty sight," Alan commented, but he was looking at Josie, not the city lights.

They reached the ranch drive, listening to some Alan Jackson tunes on a CD, both of them were humming and singing along. Alan pulled the pickup up to Josie's cabin. It was late, the Mexicans had turned the Spanish music down by now, they were sound asleep.

"I'd invite you in for a nightcap," Josie started. "But…"

Alan interrupted her. "Not yet. Not tonight. Soon…but not yet," as he leaned over to kiss her.

"Are you a mind reader, too?" Josie asked.

Alan grinned, opened his truck door to bright light, walked around to her door, opened it and walked her to the cabin door. He gave her a tight hug, leaned back and tipped his head to touch his lips to her tender, soft lips in a slow, long kiss. He stepped back, tipped his cowboy hat to her, and told her goodnight, and went for his truck. She stood on the porch of the cabin, watching him drive away and up to his ranch house at the top of the hill.

Someday, she thought to herself. *Someday,* she hoped in her heart.

Chapter 11

The weekend was a slower time at the Dream Catcher Ranch. No formal riding, Pancho and Chico did morning chores and cleaned stalls, then they got the major part of the day to themselves until chores at 6 p.m.. Bob, Digger and Josie shared weekend duties. One person took their turn to turn stall horses out in the arenas to play, check pasture water tanks, and any personal riding or odd jobs around the barns. It was a casual and relaxed time on the weekends at the ranch.

This weekend it was Josie's turn to work. She didn't mind, she could spend more time with Hope, more time with her dog, Maverick, and more time kicking around ideas of potential plans for the ranch that she wanted to talk to Alan about. Josie headed to the barn around 9:00 to look things over, and kick out a few colts to the pens and arenas. She put three two year olds out in the indoor arena. As she slammed the gate closed, it was like fireworks went off. The colts bolted, running out of control, bucking and farting, kicking up their heels and nearly running into each other. Maverick watched from the gate, barking loudly and running back and forth along the gate, just to antagonize the colts that needed no incentive to buck and run harder. Fast stops, fast pivots, the colts circled the arena trying to out-race each other.

"They're feeling good," Alan's voice was loud as he walked up to the gate. Reaching out, he softly put his hand on her back.

"Good morning," Josie said as she turned to face him, their bodies barely touching.

"Good morning to you," Alan replied in an easy-going voice as he gazed at her lovely eyes. "What's the game plan for today?" he asked.

"I'm pretty flexible," Josie answered. "I know the boss, and I was hoping to hang out with him some today."

Alan's eyes brightened, and lips smiled as he looked at her. "That can totally be arranged," he said as he pulled her in close for a delicate kiss.

"Wanna ride out to check water tanks?" Josie asked.

"You bet," Alan replied.

They saddled up Hope and Bozo, and with the Corgi following behind, they rode out at a walk toward the west pasture.

"I really enjoyed last night," Josie stated.

"Me too," Alan agreed. "I can assure you there's plenty more of that to come."

"Excellent," Josie answered, smiling as she watched a big hawk circling right above them.

After an hour's ride, they reached the tank in the west pasture—nearly 80 acres of pasture, some rock, some cactus and lots of hills. The sky was bright blue and the sun warmed them—nearly eighty degrees. The setting was peaceful, the horses were relaxed as Alan softly sang a gospel song as they rode along. At the top of the hill, they could gaze down on the seventy-five head of longhorns grazing in the field. They were magnificent! A symbol of the old west. A symbol of a true cowboy's ranch. A symbol of Texas. Alan's longhorns had their heritage traced back to the King Ranch herd. That was just incredible to Josie. The coat colors were amazing—black spots on gray, brindle brown with stripes, others with red specks on white hair. Josie decided there were no ugly longhorns. They were all beautiful. Oh, the horns! They looked so heavy and they were so huge, she had to wonder how the cow was able to lift its head. The tips looked sharp as a knife. But the longhorns didn't seem to mind. The regal beasts just kept grazing and slowly moving, oblivious to the onlookers.

"They live off air, I think sometimes," Alan said. Josie looked at him, puzzled. "They can be in a field of nothing but cactus and find a way to stay looking good, finding that little blade of grass that grows nearly under the cactus. And they can eat it, without getting cactus needles in their noses. Pretty smart old longhorns."

After checking the tanks in both the west and center pastures they rode back to the barn. No need to check the east pasture, it had a big stream running through it, always with plenty of water flowing in it.

Back at the barn, Josie took the colts in the arena back to their stalls, one by one. She turned another set of fillies out, watching them as they loved the play time and tore around, too. These fillies were not running nearly as wild and fast as the first batch of colts, since the temperature had warmed up and the fillies were not as eager to run and heat up.

Alan found some sweeping to do in the office. Josie made her way in there, too.

"How about steaks on the grill tonight?" Alan asked.

"Wow, sounds awesome," Josie responded.

"Leave a note for the Mexicans to put the fillies in and let's head up to the house now," Alan replied

"Can do!" Josie shouted.

Alan, Josie and Maverick jumped in his golf cart and meandered slowly up the ranch road to the big house.

"Got something to ask ya," Alan said. Josie gave him a curious look.

"Got a longhorn cattleman convention in two weeks in Dallas, wonder if you'd be interested in going with me."

Silence. Josie's expression was blank. A long several minutes of silence, until she cleared her thoughts and finally responded.

"Welllll," Josie said, looking down at her boots, not wanting to make eye contact, "I do have that weekend off!" she perked up. Her eyes intensely fixated on his as she gave a big grin and threw her arms around his neck. "I'd love to go!" she giggled with glee.

"Done deal," Alan replied with a tender kiss to her lips.

Alan stopped the cart in the circle drive by the waterfall in the courtyard of the huge two story ranch house.

"This is magnificent," Josie said, almost not believing her eyes at the breathtaking close-up view of the sprawling ranch home. This was the biggest house she'd ever seen.

"Don't be intimidated, Jos, a house can be real empty and worthless when there's not happiness in it," Alan said with a slightly grimaced face. She gave Alan a quick glance. He took her arm to escort her inside to show her the house. Her eyes widened as she saw open ceilings with large oak beams, huge antler chandeliers hanging over the massive rustic oak dining room table. The area was simply stunning.

They walked toward the open kitchen area full of big rustic, western cupboards, each cupboard door boasting a large bronze western star encircled with lariat rope in the center of the door. There were state-of-the-art appliances and massive, gold-flecked, black granite countertops. It featured a big granite island and four bar stools in the middle of the large area.

"Very impressive," Josie commented, somewhat dazed at the majestic home.

"I planned the layout of the house myself and had it built about ten years ago," Alan stated. "It's a dream house for me—actually the entire ranch is a dream…but a dream has no heart and soul to it if you can't share the dream *with* someone." Josie nodded that she understood. They continued the tour.

The living room, featuring rustic oak, ranch-style furniture of overstuffed leather cowhide chairs and couches with brass nail-head trim, showcased a huge mesquite wood coffee table with streaks of turquoise flecks inlaid throughout the wood. The exquisite table nearly took Josie's breath away. She stared at it for some time, not speaking, just staring at the beautiful one-of-a-kind table. Large, full length windows surrounded the entire house with 360-degree, panoramic views. Josie stopped several minutes, taking deep calming breaths as she took in the display of scenery.

Alan showed her the big office area full of vintage and modern guns, and pistols displayed on the old, red, barn board walls. There were massive locked safes full of guns. The dark oak floor lightly squeaked as they proceeded around the room taking in all the sights. The mounted deer heads and longhorn racks of various size horns were proudly displayed throughout the room. Josie stopped to admire an especially long set of horns. The pair continued down the hall to the guest bedrooms, then up the stairs to the master suite, bath and closets. Even the stairs were one of a kind, with rough-cut, open-back, oak steps and wrought iron hand rail with vintage steel wagon wheels welded right into the railing.

Josie put her hands to her mouth and gave a slight gasp the first time she viewed the fabulous master bedroom full of western rustic cedar chairs in a log cabin style. She walked further in the room just to touch the beautiful cedar chair. With light colored wood on the outside, and the red cedar glow of the center, the chair showcased the incredibly soft chocolate Brazilian leather cowhide of the seat and back. Paired with a brightly colored, striped Navajo fabric pillow, this chair was something she has only seen in magazines. She just had to sit in the chair, it was so inviting. As she sat, she ran her hands along the smooth armrests, as if caressing them with a gentle touch. Alan, watching from the doorway smiled at her childlike reaction. Josie had taken it all in, but still could not quite believe what she was seeing in Alan's home. The house boasted quality construction, upscale western lifestyle furnishings and full length windows with panoramic views of Hill Country. Josie put her right fingers over her left arm and pinched herself. Alan, watching her closely, gave a soft chuckle to himself. They proceeded back to the spacious living room, Josie stopping to admire more of the view out the large windows.

"A person can see for a million miles up here," Josie said.

"Well, I'm not sure about that, but you can see for at least three counties," Alan replied.

She noticed the large overhangs off the roof that protected the rooms most of the day from the hot summer sun.

"I bet the sunrises are beautiful from in here," Josie stated.

"You'll have to see that for yourself," Alan says back to her, with an intense stare of hope that she would want to share this with him someday.

"Let's go out on the porch and have a cold one," Alan suggested.

"Oh, damn fine idea, let's go," Josie said. They made their way down to the kitchen, grabbed two cold beers, and Alan set two big ribeye steaks from the freezer out on the countertop to thaw. They went out to the sprawling porch, nearly half the length of the house and partially overhanging a drop-off hillside that looked straight down for sixty feet to a valley stream below. Alan sat down on a big chaise lounge chair, legs apart, and encouraged Josie to come sit between his legs. She grabbed her beer, sat in front of him and leaned back on his chest. They both put their legs up on the oversized chaise chair. Hearing cows bawling, some birds chirping and an occasional squirrel cackling, it was a beautiful peaceful place.

"What would you think about sharing some of this beauty with others?" Josie asked.

Alan sipped his beer and thought a bit. "What have you got in mind Josie?" he asked her.

"What if we started a therapeutic riding program for less fortunate kids and adults, using older broke horses, and gave them a chance to ride," she presented her idea to Alan.

He thought a bit, sipping more beer, then replied, "When can we start?"

"Really?" Josie asked, as she sat straight up in the chair and turned to look at him. "You'd do it, just like that?"

"Sure," he said with a big smile. "Tell me the details while I cook the steaks," Alan told her, as he held his beer bottle up for a toast. She gladly clicked her bottle into his.

With the grill going hot, steaks sizzling, Josie rambled on and on about the idea of having a dozen older, really good broke horses, inviting handicapped children or adults to come to the ranch to groom the horses and ride if they are able. They would probably need to work with the Goodwill organization, or another type of program to find the clientele. Josie went on the explain to Alan about building a big ramp, so if they're in a wheelchair they could go up the ramp for easier mounting on the horses. She talked about having plenty of helpers to assist them in mounting and dismounting and helpers to lead the horse and walkers to follow beside the rider to help if there were any problems.

"Love it!" was all Alan would say to everything Josie talked about. He continued, "Why don't you start looking for the right kind of horses next week."

She looked at him straight in the eye, "Why don't we start looking for the right kind of horses next week," Josie said.

"Umm," replied Alan, "very good plan."

As they ate the delicious, juicy steaks at the patio table, while watching the golden sun set lower in the sky, they continued making plans for the events to come to the ranch.

"I'd like to keep Digger riding colts, so we could have several good futurity prospects," Alan presented. "We can sell some of the yearlings, keep the best six or so, move them up to the pens just south of the mare motel. The broke horses can be in the small pasture by the lane for turn out, and in the mare motel stalls when the kids come to ride," he continued.

Alan got up and went to the kitchen for more beers. "I'll research the internet to find some other folks that are doing this type work to visit with them and get plans and ideas for what needs to be done," Alan told her. The pair moved back to the oversized lounge chair with Alan leaning back on the cushion, Josie leaning back on Alan.

"We've got plans," Alan said.

"Yes, we sure do," Josie replied, tipping up the Lone Star.

They'd talked enough. The last sliver of the crimson ball sun was slipping behind the far ridge of trees. They finished the beers, it had grown darker, and Alan reached for a blanket on the back of the chair by his head, tossed it over Josie's legs and pulled it up to her chin and draped it over both their arms. It was a beautiful night of bright gleaming stars and full Texas moon. The snuggling was intoxicating and relaxing. It was the most comfortable either of them had been for a long time. They both fell asleep.

Chapter 12

Two weeks came and went so fast Josie couldn't believe it. Life on the ranch was running smoothly. So were the tender feelings between she and Alan.

Both Alan and Josie were doing research on locating good broke horses and extra people to help to work for the special needs riding program. Bob and the barn hands had built a wheelchair ramp. Everyone was excited about the plans for the therapeutic riding facility, and eager to take part. Josie even got corporate sponsors to donate funds to buy helmets for the riders, grooming supplies and brushes. It was all coming together. Even community folks were getting involved. They were hoping to start the program next month.

The weekend of the Texas Cattleman's Convention was close. Alan, Josie and Maverick, the dog, left Thursday morning from Hill Country headed up I-35 to Dallas. They left a day early, before the convention started, with hopes of purchasing horses. They pulled a big gooseneck horse trailer behind the dually pickup truck. They specifically wanted to check out good broke horses in the Dallas and Gainesville area. Gainesville was known as the best Quarter Horse country in the United States, having the most elite group of trainers and largest number of horses of all disciplines. There were reined cow horse trainers, cutting trainers, reining horse trainers and western pleasure trainers all located in that zone.

Listening to country songs, the miles passed quickly for the couple headed to north Texas.

"Can't believe we're going to Dallas!" Josie exclaimed excitedly.

"Ever been there?" Alan questioned.

"Just been through it on the interstate, never downtown," Josie replied.

"I just want you to have a good time all weekend," Alan responded.

Josie gave him a big grin as she nodded her head eagerly and replied, "Ohhhhhh, I think I will!" After a brief hesitation, she snickered and said, "I *know* I will!"

They had planned to stop at a friend's ranch between Aubrey and Gainesville before heading into Dallas. They pulled into the Chown Ranch with enthusiasm and high expectations, and were not disappointed. They spent most of the day, rode a total of twenty horses, and picked six of the best to buy. Robert, the owner and head trainer, knew of two more geldings that should be considered as additions to the Dream Catcher Ranch, now that he knew exactly what Alan and Josie were looking for. He would make arrangements for them to be in Gainesville at his place when Alan and Josie were coming to pick up the others they bought. They left their trailer and newly purchased horses for picking up on their return after the Dallas convention.

On to Dallas it was. The city was big and intimidating to Josie. Tall buildings blurred by on eight lanes of traffic, all going at a break-neck pace. Alan had no trouble negotiating the fast-paced interstate full of speeding cars and big pickup trucks. Josie noticed that nearly every pickup truck's driver was wearing a cowboy hat...*just so western*, she thought. She loved it!

They reached the site of the convention headquarters just before dark, the luxurious Omni Hotel. It was *gi*-normous! Josie had to bend her neck to look out the window to see the top of the skyscraper. Alan parked the pickup right at the front door along the busy street with traffic flying by. A bellman immediately met them, opened their doors, escorted them out of the vehicle and took their bags, as Maverick jumped out of the truck close behind. Another man, obviously a hotel employee by his uniform, took the keys from Alan and drove the pickup to an underground parking garage.

"Wow," Josie exclaimed "This is uptown! This country girl might not be ready for the big city!"

Alan chuckled, "Sure you are!" he said confidently as he gently took her elbow in his hand and escorted her inside. Alan was on one side of Josie, Maverick on the other, as they opened the doors to enter the stunningly beautiful lobby.

Their cowboy boots clicked off their steps loudly, as did the dog toenails on top of the handmade, designer Italian tile floors. They briskly entered the grand hotel lobby full of marble pillars, wall size western murals, and a giant mahogany check-in counter. They proceeded to the counter, as Josie awkwardly took in all the luxurious sites, her head and eyes turning many different directions to see it all.

"May I help you, sir?" the clerk asked.

"Alan Sutcliff, here for the convention." Alan replied, looking directly at the clerk.

"Yes, sir. Your reservation is right here, sir," the clerk said as he looked up from his computer at Alan and Josie.

"Was that one room or two?" the clerk asked.

Alan and Josie quickly glanced at each other's eyes.

"One!" they both chimed together in unison.

"Very good," the clerk responded. He ordered the bellman to take the bags as Josie, Alan and Maverick followed him to the glass-doored elevator surrounded in bright lights, and rode silently up to the fourteenth floor.

Entering the stately room, they immediately acquired the delightful scent of fresh flowers. There was a big vase of mixed, spectacular, fresh wildflowers on the table. The large, grand suite had every necessity of home with a big screen TV, a living room with western decor and a mini kitchen. There were glass French doors that opened to a magnificent bedroom. The bed was huge...*bigger than king size*, Josie thought, and raised extra high off the floor. It had mahogany pillars for bedposts and the bed was covered in puffy, down-filled, pristine white comforters. There was even a pet bed for Maverick. Josie admired the amazing accommodations, standing in the center of it all, turning slowly, 360 degrees.

"Can I get you anything else, sir?" the bellman asked Alan.

"No, this will be fine," Alan replied as he gave the bellman a $20.00 tip.

Josie took one look at Alan, kicked her cowboy boots off so fast they flew up in the air nearly hitting her in the head, then ran for the bed and jumped in it rolling around. She stood up and jumped up and down on the bed like a child on a trampoline, giggling and laughing, her long hair bouncing high, the bed in more disarray with every jump. Maverick on the floor is barking loudly, wishing he was part of the excitement up on the bed. Alan just stood there laughing at her, then he went to the bar to mix them drinks while still keeping an eye on her.

"This is *awesome!*" Josie declared. When she finished jumping, she gave one last bounce, landed on her butt in the center of the bed, then shimmied her legs over to the edge and off the bed to have a drink with Alan.

"Glad you like it, cowgirl," Alan softly remarked as he looked into her limitless dark eyes and reached for the back of her neck, pulled her in close for an intimate kiss followed by a strong chest to chest hug.

"Are you hungry? We did a lot of riding today to work up a Cowtown size appetite!"

"Sure, I could eat a"—she hesitated— *"cow!"*

He mixed drinks in the room and they slowly sipped them. Josie gave Maverick his supper, and she and Alan exited the room to head for the lobby where the bellman signaled for a cab to take them to Dallas West End Y.O. Ranch Steakhouse, the finest dining in all of Dallas. After being seated, Josie enjoyed another Southern Comfort and water, while Alan downed two drinks of Black Velvet mixed with Diet Coke. Orders were taken and quickly followed by the delivery of delicious, grilled, *huge* ribeyes covered in mushrooms sautéed in butter. Oh, what a delight for Josie, this was a dream she was living with every sense of her being!

The couple shared small talk and giggles about the fabulous day on the Chown Ranch, the good horses they bought and the schedule of the upcoming events and meetings of the convention.

Following the exquisite meal, they caught a cab for a ride back to the hotel room. The typically long, stoplight-filled ride went unnoticed as Josie and Alan took and gave slow, deep kisses in the backseat. After arriving back at the hotel, they quickly make their way, arms locked around each other's waist, to their room. Maverick was sound asleep in his bed and did not even notice the couple entering. Alan put country music on the stereo, made himself another BV and Diet Coke, gave Josie a kiss and told her he was taking a quick shower.

She heard the shower running, took a few more sips of her drink, then opened the door to the steamy bathroom, silently undressing. She saw Alan behind the glass block wall as he washed his hair, but he did not see her. She quietly tiptoed naked into the shower, grabbed the bar of soap, and standing behind him, she reached her arms around to his chest and began lathering him up. He opened his eyes, turned and looked into her beautiful face and began kissing her soft lips, his hands moving from shampooing his head, to the center of her back. They took turns softly scrubbing each other, quietly exploring each part of the other's body, followed by a long hot rinse of the water jets beading up on their bodies. He turned off the water. They each reached for the warmed, oversized fluffy white towels just outside the shower. Alan wrapped his towel around Josie as he gently dried her tender, sun-tanned skin, while gazing into her sensuous dark eyes. He took the towel she was holding, dried himself and wrapped it around his waist. He took her hand and kindly led her to the bed, turned and removed both their towels. In their nakedness, they moved closer until skins were touching. They embraced and softly fell into bed. After hours of sweet, passionate love making they both fell asleep in each other's arms.

Chapter 13

The next day, Alan arose early to shower and get dressed for the convention series of lectures and forums that started promptly at 9:00. He made a pot of coffee and gave Josie a kiss on the forehead as he left her in bed still half asleep. He left a note that he would check back with her at noon.

Josie got out of bed, scooped up the Corgi dog to quickly return to bed. They both fall back to sleep. Around 10:00, Josie enjoyed the leisurely morning, but got up and was dressed and ready to go by noon when Alan returned.

He greeted her with a close body, lengthy hug, followed by a kiss on her cheek.

"I've got more meetings this afternoon...you need a shopping day?" he asked her.

"Sure!" she gladly replied. He tossed her two credit cards, both with her name embossed on them.

"Go have fun," Alan told her. "And there's a big banquet and ball tonight—see if they make a Wrangler ball gown in this town," he laughed.

Josie looked at the credit cards, then looked at him.

"Really?" she looked as if she might cry.

He gave her a hug and said, as he looked her right in the eyes, "I'm in it for the real deal, the long haul. I hope you are, too. So let's spend some of this stinking money before the government gets it." She grinned.

"Okay, then, works for me," Josie said.

She spent the afternoon in the Galleria shopping district, shopping, buying, and trying on clothes. She tried on fabulous dresses, blouses, jeans, and cowboy boots. She even got a facial and professional makeup sitting at Macy's. She shopped for hours until she was nearly exhausted, and headed back for the hotel, toting all the new purchases.

Alan left her a note that dinner was at 7:00 and he would meet her in the lobby. Josie dressed for the gala event, kissed her dog on the head and headed down to the grand lobby just minutes before seven. He saw her from across the lobby, where he was having drinks and visiting with friends. She wore a full-length, western designed fitted skirt, red clingy low neck top, large turquoise and silver western necklace, rhinestone studded jacket and filigree two-toned leather cowboy boots. She looked amazing. Her hair was full of bouncy waves and soft curls that billowed down her shoulders and back. He made his way across the room toward her, she saw him, and gave him a big smile. Then she turned around, so he could see the big western saddle outlined in multi colored rhinestones on the back of her new jacket.

He grinned and laughed, "How cool!" he said, as he gave her a hug.

"You look—and smell—marvelous," he told her as he leaned in for a quick kiss.

"You clean up pretty good, too," she replied, noticing his black western tuxedo and black felt cowboy hat, and handmade black ostrich cowboy boots. He offered his arm, she took it and he escorted her into the grand ballroom for the banquet and ceremony and a fairytale dream come true for a country Iowa girl.

The night progressed perfectly—a delicious supper of prime rib, steamed carrots, broccoli and cauliflower, fried okra, and Bavarian chocolate cheesecake for dessert. Dancing followed the supper and awards ceremony. Alan and Josie embraced tightly in the slow dances, and smiled confidently when they two-stepped, consumed in each other. They enjoyed the entire evening, nearly oblivious that anyone else was even in the room.

Back in the room after the dance, there was another night of heated and passionate lovemaking, then fading off to sleep in each other's arms yet again.

Sunday morning, the convention now over, Josie and Alan packed, and with Maverick, left the hotel, and headed for the Chown Ranch to pick up their new horses.

They made their way north to the Chown Ranch where they rode two more well broke geldings, a big chestnut and a palomino. Alan bought them, and paid Robert for the stock. After hooking up the trailer, they loaded all eight geldings in the big rig and headed for Hill Country in central Texas, a six hour trip home.

Both tired, it was somewhat of a quiet ride home, with occasional reminiscing about the fantastic weekend. Then Alan cleared his throat to speak.

He said "How about if you move out of the cabin?"

Josie gave a shy grin and looked at him. "Where would you have me go, Mr. Sutcliff?" she asked.

He smiled back and said, "There's a big house on the hill that needs you." He reached over and gave her hand a squeeze.

She took his hand, then kissed it and said, "It would be my pleasure." She knew this was her knight in shining armor that had come to save her.

It was a long day, and a long weekend, but much was accomplished. Much accomplished for the ranch, and much accomplished for Alan and Josie. They had formed a permanent and special bond of true love now with each other.

Chapter 14

The summer seemed to fly by so quickly. Digger had three colts riding really well, doing advanced maneuvers of spins, sliding stops, speed changes and flying lead changes. He was a great trainer, and the colts reflected that. Digger was working cows with the colts; they all had a natural instinct to control the calves. He would ride into a herd of calves, push one out by itself, then keep his horse between the cow and the herd. The horse reacted quick and skillfully, staying just ahead of the cow and preventing him from returning to the pack of calves. Other times during practice, when he had just one cow in the arena, he would rein his horse back to allow the cow to gain speed, getting ahead of the horse while running along the arena fence. Digger would then speed up his horse, pass the cow and rein his horse right into it, stopping and turning both the cow and horse in an instant.

Alan saw Digger and the colts progressing so well, he entered them in the big reined cow horse show at the Snaffle Bit Futurity in Fort Worth, held in October. Digger was excited, and confident that he could do a good job at the show, maybe place well, and maybe even get the colts sold for a high price. He'd love to experience the sales of horses that he trained, making some big money for Alan and the ranch.

Alan, Josie, Bob and the ranch hands were thoroughly enjoying the new special riding program that Josie had created. Twice a week a bus load of kids and adults would come to the ranch and spend the day taking turns brushing and riding the horses. Neither Alan or Josie ever imagined how wonderful it would make them feel to see the happiness on the faces of the special riders. For the new cowboys and cowgirls, this was their first opportunity to ever ride horseback. There were big smiles, lots of giggling, cheering and shouts of ultimate joy and happiness by the kids as they rode.

It was just as rewarding to the ranch hands and Alan and Josie. They watched as the first-time, timid riders progressed over just a few weeks to being confident, bold riders and even tossing balls from on horseback, riding tight circles around poles, and even making the horses stop and back up all on their own. All of this was such great therapy, both physically and mentally, for the kids and adults. Alan had never felt so good about something in his whole life. Even though it was entirely Josie's idea, because they were a team and worked together, they were able to create this fantastic environment for others to share. He was thrilled, and so proud of himself, of Josie and of his ranch. He was finally doing something more productive than he'd ever done in his life.

By fall, the Texas governor was aware of the Dream Catcher Ranch and all the positive riding and self-esteem building work that was going on there, and made a special trip just to visit the beautiful ranch in Hill Country.

"Josie and I have been so blessed," Alan told the governor. "We just wanted to share some of our blessings with others." Josie was so proud of Alan and all they had created together. They were a truly blessed couple, and were enthusiastic about sharing their blessings from God with others.

Chapter 15

Time had come for the trip to the big show in Ft. Worth. It was a perfect fall day, with cool temperatures in the 60s, partly cloudy skies—ideal conditions for hauling horses down the road. Digger had loaded up the fancy show horse trailer with the three best cow horses and was ready to head for north Texas. All the ranch crew was there to see him off.

"Wish me luck, everybody!" he yelled as he stepped in the Western Hauler truck, put it in gear and started to pull out of the drive.

"Go for the gold!" Bob yelled as he gave thumbs up.

Digger had his truck window down was just smiling and waving, looking as happy as if he'd won the Texas lottery.

"No *Quervo* 'til you win!" one of the Mexicans yelled.

"Good luck and give 'em hell!'" Alan hollered.

"They may not know you when you pull in…but they will when you leave!" Josie yelled.

Digger continued waving and smiling until he was well out of sight from the barn. Those left standing in the driveway could no longer hear the roar of the big truck. The excitement over for now, everyone resumed their regular jobs of working the ranch. Alan went into the office to do some book work. Bob was doing repairs in the alleyway on a stall board that was broken. Josie tended to Hope, getting her out of the stall to put in the crossties and began brushing. About an hour later, Alan came out of the office.

"Is it my imagination…or does this place seem really empty with Digger gone?" Alan questioned in a loud voice.

Both Bob and Josie spun around to look over to Alan.

Josie agreed. "I can't believe how quiet it is."

Bob commented too. "I don't have nobody to give some shit to, except the Mexicans now and most of the time they act like they can't understand English."

Josie laughed at Bob's comment.

"How about if we fly out to watch Digger show at the Futurity?" Alan asked.

"Awesome!" yelled Josie as she did a whirling dance in the barn alley.

Alan looked directly at Bob. "You looking at me, Boss?" Bob asked.

"Oh, hell yes, Bob! You helped raise these colts and that boy; wouldn't you like to go watch them at Futurity?"

"Well, Lordy be, I sure would!" Bob yelled with a giggle. "Damn, that would be great!" he confirmed to Alan.

"Well that's good, 'cause I just booked a chartered jet to take the three of us, and a Corgi dog, next week!" Cheers come from both Josie and Bob, and Maverick barked loudly while spinning around and jumping up on Josie's knee.

The week seemed to fly by. Soon it was the day for the crew to leave for the big show. Josie called old friends Marne and Sierra who were going to drive down to Ft. Worth, so they could all meet at the Futurity. Alan arranged the jet, rental car for when they got there and motel rooms at the same motel Digger was staying at, the Best Western. Almost giddy with excitement, Bob met Alan and Josie at the barn, to ride together on the drive to the airport.

"The Mexicans know just what to do for chores and such, don't they, Bob?" Alan asks

"Yes, Boss, and I got the vet stopping in every day just to look things over, and neighbor Tommy Jones is going to stop in and check on things too."

"Sounds good—let's roll!" Alan said as they pulled out the ranch drive headed for the Fredericksburg Airport.

The small Fredericksburg airport next to Lady Bird Johnson Park was frequently used by many area ranchers. Small jets and planes shuttled ranchers to larger airports at San Antonio or Austin for connecting flights, saving over an hour of driving time. Alan had hired a jet to fly all the way to Ft. Worth. The trio boarded the jet and settled in for a two-hour flight.

Flying into Fort Worth on a crisp, sunny, fall day, they viewed the fairgrounds complex where the show was held. It was a sea of motor homes, horse trailers and pickup trucks, multiple coliseums and horse barn after horse barn. After landing, they stopped at the motel to drop off luggage, then made their way to the fairgrounds in the heart of the city. The show ran nearly 24 hours a day, there were so many classes for different ages of horses and different levels of riders to participate in.

They found the stall office to look up where Dream Catcher Ranch stalls were located, and proceeded to find them. Nearing the stalls, they saw Digger putting the saddle on one of the colts, a palomino gelding named The Yello Cat. Digger looked past the colt down the alleyway and saw the trio coming in his direction.

"Heyyyyy!" Digger yelled "What a surprise!" He ran up to hug Josie and shake hands with Bob and Alan.

"Things getting boring in Hill Country, you had to come to north Texas?" Digger asked.

"Yeah, something like that," Alan grinned.

"I'm just going out to ride the colt in the warm-up pen; he shows tomorrow." Digger said.

"Well, okay then, we're gonna go watch ya, and for sure follow ya, this place is *huge*, we'd get lost in a heartbeat!" Josie answered as they all made their way to the practice arena.

There were four large warm-up practice pens open for riding, but they were all quite full of horses. Some riders were in show clothes, preparing for classes to be judged; others were riding for practice in casual attire. A few youth kids were riding in sweats or pajamas, just loping horses around the arena on a loose rein. Several cowboys were doing work in the practice pen. Digger hung with them in one area of the arena somewhat less crowded. It looked like a colossal maze of riders on horseback. Alan, Josie and Bob stood along the arena fence, nearly mesmerized watching all the riding going on. They admired the beautiful saddles and top-notch horses, especially the different riding styles, as they went by.

"You sure can tell the good riders from the poor, can't ya," Bob said, and he was right. Some riders had total control of every step and movement of their horse, others just seemed to go along for the ride wherever the horse took them.

Digger put the palomino through his warm-up paces for about 45 minutes, then left the arena, swung a leg over to step off and lead Cat back to the barn. He met with the Texas trio on the way to let them know one of the large coliseums was nearby if they wanted to go in and watch some of the show going on. They grabbed a bite to eat at a street vendor nearby and headed in to watch the show.

After sitting through five cuts of junior herd work eliminations, they made their way to the nearby building which housed the large trade show. All the large tack and western stores, metal art, western jewelry, western artists, had displays and large booths for shopping. In the center of the building were rows and rows of new horse trailers brought out to the show to display and sell. It was a shopping extravaganza! Bob lasted about five minutes, then headed back to the stalls. Alan and Josie made their way around the countless shops of western products, saddles, clothes, furniture and everything imaginable in connection with a horse.

The day was nearly done, when Josie got a call. *Sierra and Marne are here!* They all zeroed in on the stall location to meet up. Digger had the stalls cleaned, horses fed and bedded down for the night. The group decided it was time to catch up on the past and get some real food, so they jumped in the pickup trucks to head for a steak house near the motel. They enjoyed tasty meals of ribeye and porterhouse steaks at the restaurant. The evening was full of lively conversation of stories about horses, reliving the *old days* of their youth, and predictions about the big ride tomorrow. The weary cowboys and cowgirls, with bellies full, finally called it a night. They said goodbyes with great expectations and nervous anticipation, for tomorrow was show day. Sleep would be difficult with eagerness and hope simmering a slow fire deep in their soul. It would be a day full of passion, an emotional roller coaster and the show day of a lifetime!

Chapter 16

Digger was up bright and early, at the stalls by 5:30 a.m., with Bob in tow. Alan and Josie made their way to the show around 8:00. Show preparations were already underway with Bob and Digger grooming all three horses that would be shown today. A cute little bay gelding, Heza Conquistador, nicknamed Scooter, was the one Digger devoted his attention to the most, as he showed around noon in the Open Bridle Working Cow Horse. By mid-morning, Alan and Josie gave well wishes to Digger, reinforcing that no matter what, they are proud of him for representing Dream Catcher Ranch at such a prestigious event. They found seats in the pavilion, eager to watch the show.

Sierra and Marne arrived at the fairgrounds, making a cell phone call to find their way to Alan and Josie's box seats. Hugs all around, and the cowgirls reminisced about the good old days and Iowa times, and the new life Josie had in Texas. Alan excused himself to make a trip to the concession stand. This gave the girls private time to talk.

"He's *amazing!*" Sierra said to Josie.

"I really like him, Jos. What a great guy," Marne said. "It's easy to see, you've found the man of your dreams." Josie blushed and smiled.

"Can't deny that, and you two know me better than anyone," Josie said. "It's so crazy—I wasn't looking for this. It all just happened! Don't know how it happened, or why I got so lucky, but the most incredible twist of my life wasn't my plan," she smiled and continued, "but it was God's plan! All my prayers came true! I'm blessed more than I ever dreamed. And I ended up on Dream Catcher Ranch; it is all so perfect!" The girls all giggled, sharing Josie's happiness with her.

Before long Alan returned to his seat. It was time for Digger to exhibit. He was nervous, with lots of butterflies in his stomach, but confident in the good bay he was riding. The judges had chosen NRCHA Pattern 3 for all horses in today's reining portion of the competition. The reining pattern was first, followed by cow work. That's when one cow was let loose in the arena and the exhibitor controled the cow, maneuvering his horse to encourage the direction and speed of the cow.

"Next up is number 2325, Heza Conquistador, sired by Conquistador Whiz and shown by Digger Matthews," the announcer boldly said over the PA system. Digger entered the arena to begin his required reining. He trotted to the center of the arena, stopped and settled his horse, taking one quick breath before he tensely began. He clicked to the gelding and gave a slight touch of his left spur to begin a right lead. Scooter and Digger completed three circles to the right, the first two large and fast followed by one slow, small circle. The spectators immediately recognized the gelding's exceptional cadence, movement and willingness to move out on the fast circle, and how easily and effortlessly he slowed down for the smaller circle. Digger cued the gelding to a lead change by slightly bumping his right spur to the ribs, and the horse changed both forward moving legs from one side to the other, flawlessly. The pattern was repeated for the left circles, so he leaned forward in the saddle, encouraging the gelding to pick up the pace for a controlled extended gallop for two circles to the left.

The horse immediately complied. His long black mane lifted up, flying nearly in Digger's face, the horse was moving at such a fast but controlled rate of speed. Completing the two fast circles, Digger sat up straighter in the saddle and the gelding conformed to a slower gait, still loping, but much more relaxed as he completed the small circle. The crowd applauded the pair's speed transition. Digger guided the horse back to the center of the arena and cued with his spur for another lead change. The gelding stepped over to the right lead without breaking gait and continued loping to the end of the arena. Digger laid the reins on Scooter's neck, the gelding made a tight turn and loped up the center of the arena, increasing speed until nearly at the end of the arena, he was at a full gallop. Scooter had nostrils flaring and sweat beaded up on his neck. He was running as fast as he could go.

Suddenly, Digger pushed his cowboy boots forward while he softly sat back in the saddle and quietly whispered, "Whoa." Scooter obeyed and dropped his hocks and rear end in the dirt, still walking forward with his front legs for a sliding stop of forty feet. Completing the stop, the horse and rider were frozen motionless. Then Digger gave a spur cue and the gelding obeyed, doing 3 ½ spins to the right. The gelding spun his front around while his back end was stationary. He spun like a top, so fast it was hard for Digger to count. He cued to stop and hesitated, with the bay totally still, no movement. The crowd's interest had awakened at this spectacular ride and rewarded the horse and rider with cheers and clapping.

Not done yet, Digger slightly wiggled the reins, gave a spur cue and the gelding loped straight off down the center of the arena over his previous tracks. He rode past the end marker on the wall, picking up speed with every stride. Again, Digger cued with his feet, sitting back in the saddle and saying, "Whoa," and the gelding dropped his rear end into the dirt sending the dirt and dust flying all around underneath and beside him. It was difficult to even see Scooter's back legs because of the loose dirt surrounding him. The crowd cheered louder and longer as the gelding completed the stop, and then hesitated slightly before feeling the rein on his neck. Scooter quickly gave 3 ½ spins to the left. Both Scooter and Digger were breathing very hard, but there was still one more maneuver. Digger cued the gelding to lope back up the middle of the arena again. When they got past the center marker, the cowboy and gelding made one final big stop, his rear sliding plate horse shoes drug the dirt and made it fly! After the stop was complete, Digger asked for the gelding to reverse and back up. With a light touch of the rein, the little gelding backed up so fast he nearly stepped back on his extra-long black tail. He was nearly running backwards. The crowd went wild cheering, hooting and hollering.

Digger was relieved that portion of the class was over, however, then he rode Scooter over toward one end of the arena and signaled for a cow to be let in. The gate opened, and a reluctant Charolais cow curiously trotted in. Scooter quickly sized up the medium size, four-hundred-pound cow. As the cow moved back and forth along the fence, Scooter moved with him. Digger reined the gelding to stay in a parallel line with the cow—they appeared almost to be dancing. As the cow moved, the horse moved. When the horse got slightly ahead of the cow, he stopped it, and the pair made a 180-degree turn to the opposite direction. The cow galloped fast, but the horse galloped even faster to get ahead of the cow. Just then the horse instinctively stopped the cow in its tracks. The horse had the breeding, the genetics, to know exactly what the cow moves would be. Scooter planted his rear feet, executed a quick 180-degree spin so fast Digger nearly came out of the saddle, even though he was hanging on to the horn.

The crowd noise of whistles, cheers and loud clapping was almost deafening, but Scooter and Digger, diligently continued working the cow at a high rate of speed. Near the corner of the arena, Digger held the gelding back slightly to let the cow get ahead as the pair ran down the long wall of the arena. The cowboy and horse were taking the cow down the fence. Nearly at the end of the arena long wall, the cowboy rode hard and pushed the gelding ahead of the cow and in one motion quickly reined the gelding's shoulder right toward the cow's head. Both the cow and the horse did an immediate stop as the horse rolled back right into the cow. The quick cow turned and darted the other way down the fence. Digger ran his horse fast to chase down the cow, getting up to the cow's head, then at break-neck speed, he reined the little gelding back into the cow and the pair made an immediate left turn. The cow hit the wall with a loud bang. The rider had successfully turned the cow on the fence both directions. As the cow and horse turned the third time, the pair ran down the fence the opposite way; however, this time Digger rode right up beside the cow and maneuvered the cow toward the center of the arena pushing it into running a small, tight circle.

The crowd had really gotten into the ride with the non-stop cheering and shrill whistles. After circling the cow to the left, Digger pulled the gelding up slightly with the reins, and asked him to move behind the cow and go to the other side of the cow. Both horse and cow were eye to eye, moving at a fast gallop. Digger and his horse tightly circled the cow to the right.

An air horn piercingly honked, Digger reined the gelding back to a stop and the ride was over. Now it was up to the three judges to make their decision.

As the gate on one end of the arena was opened, the cow exited. Digger and Scooter jog-trotted their way to the opposite end of the arena, where the next rider awaited his turn.

The announcer proclaimed that Digger and Scooter scored a 224 under the three judges for the rein work. Scoring is from 60 to 80 points. The average score is 70 points per judge, or a 210 average score for three judges, so Digger proudly knew he had been recognized by the judges for his above-average maneuvers. Then the announcer gleefully declared Digger had scored a 228 on the cow work! His combined score is 452, a fantastic ride and score for the rookie pair!

Digger had a big grin on his face as he left the arena. He knew that Scooter did his very best and he was proud of him. As he exited and stood outside the pavilion, several cowboys approached him immediately.

The rapid questions from the interested cowboys were, "How's he bred?"– "Who owns him?" – "Do they want to sell?" Digger was overwhelmed with the interest and response Scooter had created. He visited with several cowboys as Alan and Josie approached, stood nearby and listened as he bragged up the gelding, and the ranch, and the next set of two-year-olds he has started. Digger was very proud. Two cowboys gave him their business card and asked that he contact them as soon as he got a chance.

A good looking, tall, blonde cowgirl and her daughter waited patiently until all the other potential buyers had gone. The blonde introduced herself as Becky Dvorak and her teenage daughter was Hannah. They were from Iowa, and Josie remembered seeing them at the Quarter Horse shows in Des Moines. They were very interested in purchasing Scooter for Hannah to show in the youth reining and ranch riding events. Digger suggested they go back to the stall for him to unsaddle, and they could visit more about the possible sale. Digger loosened the cinch, then offered Hannah the reins to lead Scooter, while Digger and Becky followed them back to the stall. Alan, Josie and Bob followed closely behind too, optimistic about the possible sale.

Quick negotiations and Scooter had new owners, the Dvorak cowgirls. He would be Iowa bound in two days. Alan had a $65,000 promise and handshake from Miss Becky that a cashier's check would be handed over when the gelding left the show grounds. The gals gave Scooter a big hug, Hannah even gave him several kisses, whispering to him that she loved him and couldn't wait to take him to Iowa and give him a great home. They said their goodbyes and left the stall area, to return to watch the remainder of the class in the pavilion.

Alan and Josie were ecstatic about the sale! Digger and Bob were amazed at what just happened. Scooter would get a new home with some really nice cowgirls, Alan just made a good chunk of money, and Digger's fantastic ride would surely make a big splash in the cow-horse horse world!

"You get a $6,500 bonus check for this one, Digger," Alan informed him.

"Holy cow!" exclaimed Digger. "Really?"

"Well, sure," Alan said. "Your efforts deserve a reward."

Everyone was in high spirits, including Bob, but Alan didn't want to leave him out.

"Bob, you're part of this deal too," Alan relayed. "Figure on a $2,500 bonus on your next check."

"Really?" Bob says on cloud nine. "What for? What did I do?"

"Well," Alan gave a smile and said, "just for being you, Bob. Just for being you!" Everyone was thrilled, recapping Scooter and Digger's run.

By 2:00 p.m. the class was completed and the announcer was calling for specific entry numbers to return to the arena for awards. Digger and Scooter's number was called. Digger quickly saddled Scooter up, pushed his cowboy hat down tight, stepped into the stirrup and loped off to the arena. Josie, Alan and Bob quickly made their way to the pavilion, too. The announcer began reading the places starting at 10th place. As the horses pulled out when their number was called, the only two left standing in the arena were Digger on Scooter and another cowboy on a Metallic Cat gelding. Scooter's number was called. Dream Catcher Ranch had been awarded 2nd place out of the class of 100 entries. As the results were read over the loudspeakers, shouts of joy abounded from the Dream Catcher ranch crew. They all agreed this was the icing on the cake! How great that the little bay gelding placed so well.

Digger rode forward to accept the awards, a silver headstall, custom made wooden stirrups and a check for $20,000. The photographer snapped a few photos and Digger exited the arena, rushing to return to the barn to get his next horse ready for the following class.

Digger started preparing the next horse to show, a palomino gelding named Yello Cat, by leading him out of the stall to put in the crossties and brush. He pulled on his lead rope; the gelding didn't want to move. Digger pulled harder; the gelding reluctantly followed. As he came out of the stall, a definite limp on his hind leg was apparent.

"Oh, shoot!" Digger yelled. All heads turned and looked at him.

"Yello Cat hurt himself in the stall!" he continued, watching the gelding put no weight on the right hind leg. He stood on the toe of his hoof.

A quick inspection of the stall confirmed big gouges and marks on the side wall where the Cat evidently rolled over into the wall. He got stuck and had to get himself free by kicking and pushing back from the wall while lying on his back.

"He got cast," Digger said sadly. Bob quickly came to his aid, takes the gelding from Digger and went to the wash rack to run cold water on Yello Cat's leg. Nothing to do now but scratch the class, and ice him down. Disappointed, they all agreed that was all that could be done for Cat at the Futurity. This show was done for him.

"Just put it out of your mind and get the big chestnut gelding, Pardner, ready, Dig," Josie encouraged. "We have to take the bad with the good…seems today we're getting both."

"Yeah, I'll try," Digger said, nodding his lowered head.

Digger opened the stall of the other gelding and brought him out into the alleyway. Josie helped brush and groom him and quickly Digger threw his Martin cowhorse saddle up on the 15'2-hand tall gelding, bridled him then led him out of the barn, stepped on and went to the warm up pen.

"Don't forget your number," Josie yelled.

"Oh, thanks, Jos, can you bring it up to the pen?" Digger asked.

"Sure, meet ya up there," Josie replied. Digger continued riding up the street to the warm-up pen, Alan and Josie walking quickly, close behind.

Bob continued working on the hurt gelding, then put Cat back in his stall, with a rub on the neck and telling him it's not his fault. Bob hastily made his way to the show pavilion.

With every step, the friends were dwelling on the disappointment of the injury, and struggling to put it out of their minds. They tried to focus instead on Pardner, being quite optimistic in the talent of the next horse Digger was riding. Very Smart And Light, nicknamed Pardner, was an eye-appealing, deep red chestnut colored, perfectly proportioned horse. He epitomized the ideal Quarter Horse with his conformation, well-toned heavy muscling, powerful shoulders and hindquarters, accented with a long pencil neck and fashionable, chiseled head. Digger had trained him not only as a reining horse, but also as a cutting horse, highlighting his natural ability to work a cow. Today he would be shown in the feature class, the Open Cow Horse Futurity. He was a versatile horse and he had a unique combination of speed and strength. One if his best attributes was his laid-back personality. His calm nature, combined with exceptional athleticism, made him an outstanding cow horse. Even so, the Texas crew was full of tension, anxiety and questions. *Does Pardner really have what it takes to exceed at this level of competition? – Can Digger get through this complicated, detailed pattern to perfection? – Will they draw a good cow? – Are Pardner and Digger ready to give it their all?*

As Alan, Josie, and Bob made their way to the warm up arena, they were silently thinking about these questions. Digger reined the big gelding into the practice pen, his head swimming with the pattern details, laying out each maneuver in his mind. He tried to concentrate on what he needed to do, rather than the unknown problems that could arise. However, he knew things could go wrong very fast in any cow horse ride.

In top-notch condition, the big chestnut stoically presented himself in the warm-up pen. He was alert, confident and anxiously awaiting any command his rider would give him. However, the gelding suddenly felt the nervousness in Digger's legs as he bumped them against his ribs. He sensed tension in the reins. The horse knew something big was looming.

Would the horse and rider be up to the biggest challenge of their show career?

Chapter 17

At the warm up pen, Digger received more good luck wishes from Josie, Alan and Bob. Josie safety-pinned the number on the saddle blanket and the threesome headed in to find their good box seats. This was a limited three-year-old cow horse class, with $250,000.00 total prize money paid out. $150,000.00 was the first-place winnings, along with a horse trailer, custom western hauler truck, hand painted picture of the winner and a year's supply of Lifeline horse supplement.

Another large class, it had been going for over an hour already. They sat watching two hours of ride after ride of well-trained horses, professional trainers getting fabulous maneuvers from them.

"Number 3777 is next in the arena," the announcer said. "Very Smart And Light is sired by Very Smart Remedy, shown by Digger Matthews, Fredericksburg, Texas, and owned by Alan Sutcliff and Dream Catcher Ranch," the announcer continued.

Alan and Josie fidgeted nervously as Digger entered the arena on the good-looking chestnut, his long mane and tail flowing attractively with every step as he moved. The colt trotted to the middle of the arena on loose romel rein and stopped directly facing the judges. Digger picked up the rein ever so slightly, cued with the left spur for the gelding to begin on a right lead. Leaning forward, he encouraged Pardner to extend the lope, making perfectly sized, large, fast circles, covering half of the big arena. Then he sat back ever so slightly, more straight up in the saddle, so the gelding recognized the cue to slow lope as he made another circle half the size of the first two, and much slower and relaxed.

Digger reined the big horse to close the circle, and keeping his shoulders straight, he cued with the right spur for the gelding to pop over to the left lead. Effortlessly, the gelding complied for a smooth execution. Digger again leaned forward, pushing his rein hand toward the gelding's floating mane for the extended lope on the two big circles. Pardner looked forward with his ears up. Diligently, he stayed perfectly between the bridle reins as he raced around the arena at break-neck speed, but staying very controlled, smooth and fluid. At the center of the arena, Digger sat back, more erect. The gelding felt that cue and instantly transitioned to a slow lope with finesse, while making a much smaller circle.

Digger found a moment to breathe.

The crowd began shrill whistles, applause and cheers for this amazing change of speeds.

Back at the center of the arena, Digger held his breath and hummed for the cue for Pardner to switch to his right lead. Sometimes a troublesome maneuver, the chestnut cleanly changed the propelling side of his body to change direction. He kept his same slow, comfortable loping pace. Digger took another breath. He continued maneuvering the big horse to the end of the arena to prepare for the run-down. When centered at the end of the large pen, Digger rode Pardner to run lengthwise through the arena. With controlled speed, the big horse traveled in a straight line. Digger barely touched the reins, as he encouraged the horse to pick up his pace. At the opposite end of the arena, Digger rolled his back in the saddle, sent his boots forward for the stop cue. Pardner responded with his hocks well under him and his head low as dirt flew all around the pair. The gelding continued the big slide with his front legs moving, back legs stopped low in the dirt. The crowd went wild over the fifty-five-foot slide!

The stop maneuver was followed by 3½ spins to the right. The gelding's back right foot was planted in the ground like he was digging a fence post hole, all the other legs flew around in motion, then stopped. Hesitation. Digger felt himself take a breath. The colt intensely listened for the next cue. Digger barely lifted the rein on the colt's neck, the gelding obeyed and loped down the full length of the center of the arena, picking up his pace on nearly every stride until they were at the far end and Digger cued for the big stop. Pardner dropped his head, rounded his back as if it was about to break in half, and almost sitting on his tail, he dropped his hocks in the dirt again for a magnificent, excessively sliding long stop of more than sixty feet. The crowd went wild once again, cheering, whistling and screaming in praise. Digger took a breath, as he straightened his saddle and hesitated. But as Digger cued Pardner into the left 3½ spins, the crowd went dead silent. Everyone was silently counting the spins to make sure the horse and rider did not overspin or underspin, which would result in a huge deduction.

One spin. Pardner had found the rhythm of doing the 360 degree turn with his inside hind quarter remaining stationary, his front legs flying around in cadence. Two spins. The hind quarters remained fixed while the front legs quickly dug in the dirt to propel the big horse around. Three spins. Pardner was still smooth; with his head low he showed perfect mobility with front end moving, back end nearly still. Digger was counting the spins as he whipped his head around to a fixed point on the arena wall with every spin to keep his balance. The horse was spinning so fast, Digger could barely focus his eyes on the fence. One-half spin and *stop*. Digger and Pardner finally achieved the required one thousand, two hundred sixty-degree spin, and were now facing back toward the center of the arena. The crowd praised the outstanding spin maneuver with more cheering. The noise in the arena was deafening. Everyone in the stands was clapping and joyously yelling at the flawless reining ride.

One maneuver left to go.

Digger rocked just a bit in his saddle, getting his body in position, and letting his horse settle. He took another deep breath, noticing his mouth was so dry he was not sure he could even give the clicking sound for Pardner to go.

He gave a spur cue, barely mustering a kiss sound for the big horse to lope off, and back down the arena the pair raced at Pardner's fastest gallop. Once again, the cowboy cued with his boots going forward as he leaned back deep in the saddle and said, "Whoa." The dirt flew everywhere. This time Pardner slid nearly seventy feet! His hocks and lower legs completely under him almost like he will tip over backwards, yet in complete control of this high-level maneuver. The big horse skid further than ever! Just like his other stops, Pardner dug two parallel lines in the dirt with his special sliding plate horse shoes as he completed the maneuver. He finally came to a complete stop, and without hesitation backed up, straight, fast, but controlled. The ride was flawless! The crowd was going crazy with applause, cheers and shrill whistles of praise.

Digger hesitated just a moment, and took another breath as he reached up to push his cowboy hat down tighter on his head. He motioned for the gateman to release a cow.

Into the arena came a 450-pound Black Angus cow. This feisty cow had its tail up over its back, was running fast, looking for a place to jump the fence to get out of the arena.

Quickly moving toward the cow, Pardner made quick moves left to right as the cow did. Face-to-face, the cow and the horse began the dance. The cow moved quick to the left, the horse moved faster to stop the cow. The cow began to run the short wall end of the arena. Pardner gave a burst of speed to get ahead of the cow, while staying parallel with him some five feet away. The cow locked his legs, stopping quickly and turned to reverse his direction. Pardner followed, and with his eyes glued to the head of the cow, he dropped his front-end low to the ground and made the counter-move perfectly. The pair continued—more fast and furious head-to-head moves. The crowd was clapping with praise for the move. Pardner and Digger continued to hold the cow on the short end of the arena wall for two more minutes. Pardner was demonstrating his ability to hold the cow with his superior cow sense and natural cow-working ability. The crowd applauded and cheered loudly.

Digger realized the cow was wearing down. He held the reins tighter to allow the gelding to back off the cow, so the cow would run down the arena long fence. The cow charged along the wall, Pardner one horse-length behind, until Digger spurred the gelding to go full blast and get past the cow. As soon as Pardner's shoulders were at the cow's head, Digger reined a hard right. Pardner complied with a sliding stop, his shoulder into the cow's head and the pair made an abrupt 180-degree turn. Digger knew the extreme speed of this cow will garner bonus points with the judges.

The cow continued a run along the wall back toward its entry gate with Pardner in hot pursuit. After just passing the flag marker on the wall, Digger directed Pardner to shoulder into the cow's head to immediately stop and turn the cow to the left. Pardner had no fear as he rated himself along the wildly galloping cow. He pressed his shoulder to the cow's face as both come to a complete stop and turned, barely missing the arena wall. Digger knew he had completed turns both ways, but ran the cow down the fence for one more stop and right turn which was done flawlessly.

Then Digger and Pardner moved the cow to the open part of the arena and circled the animal both ways. The ground gave way and the cow stumbled before regaining his gallop. Pardner rated himself with the cow and as the pair were eye-to-eye, side-by-side, the big chestnut made the cow circle to the left. Digger could smell the stink of manure on the cow they were so close. After a good circle for the judges to see, Digger pulled up the reins and Pardner fell back behind the cow. The cowboy urged the horse forward faster and Pardner came up alongside the cow on the right side to push the cow into a left circle. The big horse and Angus cow were side by side. Digger heard the air horn blow, he reached down with his hand and slapped the cow on the back. He pulled the reins for Pardner's cue to stop. They were both exhausted! Digger's heart was beating so fast, it felt like it would jump out of his chest. Pardner had flared nostrils, neck and flanks were drenched in sweat, yet his big bright eyes and forward ears showed his intent and desire to do it all over again.

Everyone was on their feet, screaming and whistling and cheering so that the arena sound level felt like it would blow the roof right off. It was deafening!

Alan looked to Josie as they were both standing, clapping wildly. He said something to her, but no way could she even hear what he said, it was so loud in the coliseum.

Digger reached his hand down to pet Very Smart And Light on his sweaty neck. The gelding's nostrils seeking air, were flaring as he recovered from the strenuous workout he'd just completed. He let the gelding stand and rest a minute and then realized all the noise. Digger couldn't believe how the cheering and clapping just kept going and going and going, for several minutes, until the loudspeaker boomed with incredible words.

"A *new* high score, ladies and gentleman, and your *new leader*," the loudspeaker blared and the announcer's voice cracked as he exclaimed, "with a score of 234 on the rein work! That's *two, thirty, fourrrr!* And 240 on the cow work—that's a total of *four seventy fourrrr!*" The announcer was as excited as the crowd as he proclaimed the amazing record-

89

breaking score! The frenzied crowd got even louder and reached a new level of sound decibels. Boot stomping started with everyone stomping in unison, standing up—just going crazy! The adrenaline rush was felt throughout the entire building. Digger tried to hold back tears, but he was too choked up. He couldn't believe—*himself*—what just happened! He stepped off and with one rein, led Pardner out of the arena, lifting his hat off his head and waving it to the crowd, while wiping back tears with his shirt sleeve. Most of the audience started crying too, especially all the women. Most of the men pulled out hankies, were sniffing and had swollen, glossy red eyes with tear drops sliding out the corners. What a moment to share!

Digger put his black felt cowboy hat back on his head, and using his index finger he pointed skyward, thanking Jesus for the ride he'd just been given. What a gift. What a cowboy, and *oh, what a horse*.

Alan and Josie turned toward each other for the biggest hug ever. Arms wrapped tightly around each other, they had big tears running down their cheeks. They were awestruck by what they just witnessed! Sierra and Marne were standing and hopping together. The elated pair were hugging and crying happy tears, relishing what just happened.

As Digger and Pardner neared the end of the arena to exit, the rest of the crew wiped their eyes and quickly make their way out of the box seats, along the walkway where Alan and Josie met Digger just outside the gate. Josie jumped in Digger's open arms, both crying. Everyone was crying! What a historic moment. What a moment to remember. Josie stepped back and Alan grabbed Digger's hand for a handshake, then pulled him close for a big hug.

Through Alan was crying he mustered the words, "You done us proud, boy, you done us proud!" Digger couldn't even talk with the big lump still in his throat, tears in his eyes and running down his cheeks. He just kept affirmatively shaking his head in disbelief.

Josie led the gelding out of the building, into the cool October night, with a swarm of people following them. Many folks circled the gelding, and Alan and Josie, offering generous handshakes and heartwarming congratulations. People were talking loudly, laughing and joyously reliving the incredible show of horsemanship and horse talent they had just seen.

Just outside the coliseum, Digger saw Bob leaning against the wall, smoking a cigarette. Digger walked toward him. Bob stomped out the cigarette, met Digger and extended a hand for a handshake. Digger looked closely into Bob's eyes. He'd been crying. Bob wrinkled his face, trying so hard not to, but he burst deeper into tears.

"I ain't never seen nothing like that!" Bob sobbed big tears, forcing the words out, while burying his head on Digger's shoulder. "I ain't never seen such a perfect ride!" Digger and Bob embraced, hugged and cried together. Alan and Josie started laughing, as they were still crying; just watching Bob cry so hard made everyone laugh.

Chapter 18

The entire bunch from Dream Catcher Ranch were all exhausted, including people and horses. What an emotional ride—a heart stopping, incredible ride. Suddenly, multitudes of people were closing in on Digger and the gelding with well wishes, congratulations, handshakes and hugs. People he didn't even know were coming up to him from every direction, just to tell him that was a phenomenal job, what an amazing ride, they'd *never* seen anything like it.

The crew tried to make their way back to the stall, but so many people kept stopping to talk to Digger, it seemed to take an hour to get back there. Finally, they reached the stall area. The cooler of beer and whiskey came out of the tack stall. It was time to party! The beer tasted so good and the whiskey went down so smooth. Alan spun the top off the large bottle of Crown Royal and threw the cap over his shoulder. Everyone was laughing, smiling and reliving the happy chain of events, still not believing what just took place.

An older, lightly-graying-haired cowboy did a slow walk toward the stalls. He was dressed to perfection with heavy starched jeans and shirt, black felt cowboy hat and black ostrich boots. He reached Alan, Josie, Digger and Bob and introduced himself as George Bush. He asked who was the owner of the horse, and Alan told him that he was.

The gentleman cleared his throat to speak.

In a Texas southern drawl he said, "I'll offer you $250,000 for the horse, and would be interested in talking to your trainer about hiring him for $150,000 a year, all perks included."

Digger nearly choked on his cold beer. Alan thought a minute, then looked at Digger.

"I can't speak for the trainer, but I'll consider that price for the horse. He is a gelding."

"I know," said Mr. Bush. The elegantly dressed cowboy turned and looked at Digger for an answer.

Digger looked at Alan.

"Oh, wow!" is all he could say. "Can I sleep on it?" Digger asked.

"Oh, sure, here's my card. I'd love to have you and that horse at my Midland, Texas, ranch. Call me tomorrow," George said as he shook hands, turned and walked away.

After Mr. Bush was out of sight, the foursome all looked at each other, with jaws dropped. Digger busted out snorting and laughing.

"Was that *really* him?" Josie asked.

"Oh, yeah, it was," Alan informed her.

"What ya gonna do, son?" he asked, looking at Digger.

"Oh, hell, Boss, can I at least wait to see if I win the class?" Digger responded. Everyone laughed. Alan handed everyone another shot of Crown and an ice-cold beer.

An hour later, an announcement was made over the loudspeaker in the barns and arenas calling for ten different numbers to return to the arena. Digger heard the announcer call for number 3777 to please report to the arena. Digger put the bridle back on the big gelding who'd been munching hay but was still saddled, standing in his stall. He pulled the girth up tight and led the gelding out of the barn, followed by Alan, Josie and Bob. He stepped up on the gelding and loped off to the entrance of the coliseum, giving a glance back over his shoulder and a big smile. The others took a shortcut to the arena, using the spectator entrance. A four-horse, 4-Star, shiny aluminum horse trailer was being pulled into the arena by a new, white, Chevy dually Western Hauler pickup. On the top of the trailer was written NRCHA FUTURITY CHAMPION. The show committee was carrying out a new engraved saddle and a three-foot by six-foot replica poster of a check made out for $150,000.00.

Ten contestants stood side-by-side, with horse butts to the arena wall. Some were anxiously waiting, others were visiting with spectators or other contestants. The announcer began to read the placings, starting with tenth place. He continued the countdown until there were only two horses and cowboys left in the arena. One was Digger on Very Smart And Light, the other was Robert Chown on Smartascat. The announcer cleared his throat and called for Robert to ride forward and receive his Reserve Champion awards. Robert leaned over, gave Digger a handshake of congratulations and loped his gelding off to get his prize.

"Would contestant 3777 please ride forward, and owners please come into the arena," the announcer called amongst all the cheers and applause from the crowd. Digger loped the gelding across the arena, a slow lope, reins draped down long, the gorgeous chestnut gelding, full, long mane lightly floating in the breeze as he loped. Alan, Josie, the Corgi and Bob reached the new horse trailer the same time as Digger and the gelding. Digger pulled the gelding to a stop and the gelding naturally dropped his hip and hock for a short slide, sending the crowd into stronger cheers and applause. A photographer and assistant helped get the group lined up for a photo as the announcer spoke over the loudspeaker:

"Ladies and Gentlemen, your Futurity Champion is Very Smart And Light, sired by Very Smart Remedy, owned by Dream Catcher Ranch of Fredericksburg, Texas, and ridden by Digger Matthews. Let's give them a hand for their record breaking score of *four hundred, seventy four points!*" The crowd applauded and cheered loudly—shrill whistles could be heard too.

"Who should I make the check out to?" asked the show committee lady who was standing near the photographer as she clicked away, taking the photos.

"Make it out to Digger Matthews" Alan said.

Digger's head spun toward Alan. He couldn't believe his ears! His grin got even bigger as they all posed for pictures in front of the trailer, new saddle and the big check. What a great night! What a great life!

Bob looked at Alan in between the camera clicking off shots and exclaimed, "How the hell we getting this new rig home?" They all busted out laughing!

Chapter 19

So many memories were made on that special night in Fort Worth, Texas.

The gelding was sold to the Bush family; Digger delivered him a week after the show. Alan's theory was to make some big money, and start all over with more young prospects next year with the challenge of doing it all again.

Digger declined the amazing offer for training for the Bush's Ranch. He just loved Hill Country, Dream Catcher Ranch, and Alan and Josie too much to leave it. Jaclyn, Digger's girlfriend, moved in with him at the ranch in the trainer's house, with plans of getting married next year.

Bob drove the new truck and trailer home from Texas, Digger drove the ranch rig, following him, loaded with the new saddle and all the winning prizes and one horse to come home with, the palomino gelding that got hurt. Yello Cat recovered a month after the show. Bob got himself a girlfriend, a bubbly, younger, good looking light-haired gal named Norma who moved in his ranch house with him. She took good care of him, and he wasn't nearly so grumpy anymore.

Alan gave all the prizes won at the big show to Digger, figured if it wasn't for him, they wouldn't have gotten any of it. He used the 2nd place prize money Scooter had won, plus Pardner's big sale check, to help fund the special needs riding program at the ranch. He used that to buy more horses, making plans to invite more participants to come enjoy riding at the ranch for years to come.

Josie was so happy to reconnect with her best friends while in Texas. Both Sierra and Marne made plans to move to Dream Catcher

Ranch to help with the special riding program and various ranch duties.

"Two more Iowa cowgirls coming to Texas," Josie would say. "Now it's my friends' turn to find *their* end of the rainbow in Hill Country!" They were going to be moving into the ranch cabin the first of next year; everyone was so excited.

Alan, Josie and Maverick enjoyed each and every day on the ranch, riding together, working together, watching Digger work the young stock, fulfilling their dream of the special needs riding program and just loving life and each other.

The fall season quickly passed into winter. Alan decided to throw a big ranch Christmas appreciation party with everyone welcome to come. It was a huge event with week-long preparation—scrubbing down and cleaning walls in the barn and indoor arena, setting up 200 chairs with tables and a bar and making a stage at the end of the arena for a band. It was an enormous undertaking. Briskets were slow cooked at Cranky Franks, the barbeque place in town, then hauled out to the ranch in large warming tanks. It was a barbeque feast with all the fixings and giant plastic tanks filled with ice and beer and pop.

There were over 300 people attending the party throughout the day. There was great country music played all day long by Thomas Michael Riley and Mike Blakley. Cowboys and cowgirls packed the dance area for hours enjoying the tunes and two-stepping. There were games in the outdoor arena for kids to play. Even a dog show for the local ranch dogs to come and show their stuff in agility contests. Most folks just enjoyed sitting on the chairs in the arena, drinking a frosty Lone Star and visiting with friends and neighbors. It was a wonderful day of laughter, stories and friendships.

The week leading up to Christmas was a full day of clean up, followed by laid back, easy work in the barns with some ranch hands taking trips far away to visit families for the holidays, and those that stayed home only working a few hours a day doing basic chores.

Chapter 20

Alan and Josie planned a quiet Christmas day together on the ranch. Following chores and turning out a few horses in the arenas, they both rode in the golf cart up to the ranch house.

"Time for Christmas brunch and presents," Alan said with a glimmer in his eye.

"Oh, yeahhhhhh," Josie replied, giving him a squeeze on the leg.

As they walked into the house, they were hit with a strong smell of hazelnut coffee; they both made their way to the kitchen and Josie poured two cups adding a shot of Baileys liquor in both. Alan came out of another room, with a present behind his back. Josie reached up in a cupboard and pulled out a wrapped present with a big red bow.

"Hmmmmm," Alan said, "seems Santa Claus has been here."

"Guess so," Josie replied. "Yours first." Alan took a sip of the delicious fresh brewed coffee, sets the cup down and gently took the gift from Josie's hand. He slowly unwrapped it, finding a black leather box.

"Oh, I needed a new box," Alan said with a smile.

"Well, open the box!" Josie anxiously spoke up. "It's not just a box, there's something in it!" Alan opened it to find a beautiful wrist watch made by the jeweler at the Futurity. The black face had gold hands, complete with horses at the tip of the hands, so it appeared the horses are running as the hands swept around the face of the watch. The wristband had black reining horses inlaid in the gold band.

"It's incredible!" Alan wiggled with delight.

"Now it's your turn," Alan said. He handed Josie a long skinny box, simply wrapped in newspaper comics. She quickly opened the gift to find a new pair of soft, buckskin-colored, leather gloves.

"Oh, these are really nice," Josie replied, thankful for the gift.

"Try them on," Alan coaxed, "see if they're the right size."

"Oh, okay, sure," Josie complied.

She put the right glove on. It felt as soft as warm butter.

"They fit fine." she announced.

"Well, make sure they *both* fit," Alan encouraged.

She puts the left glove on, just started to say it's fine, too, when she froze and stopped cold. Josie was totally motionless. She quickly turned her head to look at Alan. He was absolutely glowing, grinning with a twinkle in his eye.

"What's thissss?" Josie asks as she felt a small, cold piece of metal inside the glove.

They were both silent and holding their breath. She pulled a ring out of the glove. It was the most beautiful ring she had ever seen and she was stunned!

Her hand quivered. She was holding a blue, teardrop shaped sapphire stone with diamonds inset in the gold band on both sides of the sapphire.

"Oh, my God…it's beautiful, Alan!" Josie exclaimed. She couldn't believe what she was looking at, it was so incredible, so unexpected.

"I love you, Josie," Alan said softly, as he leaned in for a kiss. "I love you, I want the entire world to know about our love; this is my love-you ring. I'm declaring it to the whole world. From now to forever, you are my partner for life."

Big tears filled Josie's eyes.

"I've never been so happy. I love you so much, Alan." She touched his face with her soft hand.

"I love you with all my soul," Alan replied. "We have so many life adventures ahead of us.

"And, cowgirl," Alan continued, "how about if we try this cow horse thing together?"

"You mean us hit the show circuit?" Josie questioned.

"Why sure," Alan replied. "We love horses, and horse shows, and really enjoy making new friends. We can show in the ranch riding and working cow horse boxing classes. You can teach me all about showing. It will be great! It can be our next dream together. Let's get some good cow horses and go have fun!"

He reached his hand out to her, she took it as the rose up together, eyes fixed on each other.

Alan whispered, "You're my world, *you* are my everything."

"Let's do this!" the pair gleefully said in unison.

They began dancing, embracing and swaying with pure, sincere eyes locked in deep comfort. They danced and swayed, slow at first, then Alan gave Josie a twirl. He pulled her in for a tender hug, then pushed her out for another twirl. The Corgi beside them jumped up and down as they embraced. They kissed with hugs, then loud laughter, then dancing, then more excited kisses. They both knew their love and lives at last were truly fulfilled.

Josie glanced up to the magical dream catcher on the wall. It was much different from any she had ever seen and stunningly beautiful. The hoop was circled in leather, with feathers and horse hair cascading down from the enchanted circle. It was full of teal colored Australian opal stones surrounding a large diamond. Josie stared at it for several minutes. With tears welling in her eyes, she realized she had truly caught her dream! The next chapter of her life could only get better. Splendid love, wonderful horses, exciting adventures. Hope, courage and passion had propelled her to reach her destiny. Her heart is in the Hill Country.

Kris Klingaman on Very Smart and Light

AQHA Superior Ranch Riding
37 AQHA All Around & Reserve All Around Championships
AQHA points in 18 Events & Grand Champion at Halter
NCHA Money Earner

About the Author

Raised on an Iowa Century family farm, Waterloo native Kris Klingaman has a genuine life-long love of animals, especially horses.

A mother of two, she had an extensive career of training and showing Paint and Quarter horses, combined with a rewarding 30-year career of professional horse judging throughout Iowa and the Midwest. Kris has loved, trained and shown many State and National

Champions including her favorites: Dainty Affects, APHA Versatility Champion, and Very Smart and Light, AQHA Performance Champion, Superior Ranch Riding, Ranch Versatility Amateur Champion, 2016 and 2017 Iowa Quarter Horse Association Open All Around Champion and High Point Performance Champion.

Kristin Jo Klingaman met the love of her life, David Alan Albrecht in 2003. He saved the last dance for her. Before retiring in 2014, Dave and Kris farmed 3,000 acres of corn and soybeans. Currently, the couple enjoy adventures together as they journey through life, living on their Fairbank, Iowa, farm, as well as their second home in Fredericksburg, Texas. Now at ages 64

and 60, surrounded by their prize-winning Quarter Horses, the couple delight in showing in the ranch riding and cow horse events at American Quarter Horse Association and National Reined Cow Horse Association shows throughout the Midwest and southern states.

Dave on Heza Conquistador
(aka Scooter)

Dave on Santa Brought Me Cash
(aka Buster)

Dave Albrecht & Kris Klingaman

Kris on Very Smart and Light with Dave at the
Iowa Quarter Horse Association Fall Classic and Futurity 2017

Made in the USA
Columbia, SC
04 December 2017